Marsha L. Marden, D.M.D.

MW01488166

BENEFICIARIES' REQUIEM

For Marsha Marden

with best wishes

BENEFICIARIES' REQUIEM

Francis M. Nevins

Mike Nevins

Five Star
Unity, Maine

Copyright © 2000 by Francis M. Nevins

All rights reserved.

This novel is a work of fiction. Names, characters, places, and incidents are either the product of the author's imagination, or, if real, used fictitiously.

Five Star Mystery
Published in conjunction with Tekno Books and Ed Gorman.

March 2000

First Edition

Five Star Mystery Series.

The text of this edition is unabridged.

Set in 11 pt. Plantin by Rick Gundberg.

Printed in the United States on permanent paper.

Library of Congress Cataloging-in-Publication Data

Nevins, Francis M.
  Beneficiaries' requiem / Francis M. Nevins. — 1st ed.
    p. cm. (Five Star mystery series)
    ISBN 0-7862-2373-1 (hc : alk. paper)
    1. Law teachers — Wisconsin — Fiction. 2. Inheritance and succession — Wisconsin — Fiction. 3. Family — Wisconsin — Fiction. 4. Wisconsin — Fiction. I. Title. II. Series.
  PS3564.E854 B46 2000
  813'.54—dc21   99-059537

For Peggy Stewart

ONE

When he drove past the WISCONSIN WELCOMES YOU sign the sky still showed streaks of blue. Ten miles down the state highway all he could see through the windshield was shades of Wagnerian gray merging into black. A tongue of lightning stabbed the horizon. The first thunderclap followed like an exploding bomb. Rain surged down on the Camry's roof. He flicked on the wipers and high beams, slowed to thirty. The windshield stayed flooded. He couldn't see if he was still on the road. Clammy with sweat he hit the emergency blinkers and hunched in the driver's seat, squinting through the tiny arc of visibility below the wiper blade which began to wobble and threaten to fly off into the woods. At the edge of his vision he saw what looked like an overpass crossing the highway and kept coaxing the Camry through water as high as its hubcaps till the shelter of the overhead crossing was above him. He parked on the gravel shoulder with the engine running and emergency lights blinking and opened the driver's side window for air. A semi roared by and drenched him. *This is insane,* he muttered to himself. *It can't work. For two cents I'd turn back and go home. Why am I doing this?*

He was doing it because he was lonely and his life was empty and because she had flown hundreds of miles to look him up and ask him. Now on this miserable Sunday morning almost a month later, with less than a hundred miles between him and the small city her ancestors had created out of wilderness, he wished he'd never laid eyes on her.

He made up his mind that once the storm let up he'd swing around and go back. If he pushed the speed limit and didn't hit more bad weather he could be home by midnight. But the woman and the plan kept tempting him. *I could stay just long enough to look the town over, check out the situation. Keep going to Dennison, leave tomorrow morning, and all I lose is one day.* A day he'd only waste moping around his condo anyway. Beyond the shelter of the overpass the upper branches of trees swayed in the wind gusts. The only sounds he could hear were thunderclaps and the drum of rain.

Highway beams glaring in his rearview mirror blinded him. He squinted his eyes shut, squirmed in his seat, focused through his glasses on another car slithering gingerly along the waterlogged road towards cover. When it slid past the Camry on the shoulder he made out that it was a dark sedan. A few seconds later it was in the open again, blending into the storm.

A few hundred feet beyond the overpass he saw the ruby glow of brake lights. The dark car halted, then with infinite caution U-turned on the flooded empty road and crawled back into the shelter of the overpass as if the driver were afraid to go farther till the storm died. Its highway beams went dark as it eased into the shoulder across from Loren. He heard steel doors open and slam shut. Two figures strode across the empty highway and approached him. Elderly ladies, each with what looked in the murk like a furled umbrella at her side. The one in the oyster-colored raincoat was short and blocky with stiffly permed iron-gray hair. The other looked smaller and frailer with thin soft white hair and a black ankle-length coat so old it seemed to shine. Were they lost? Something wrong with their car?

Then they lifted their arms in unison and Loren saw that they were carrying not umbrellas but baseball bats.

Iron Gray's first swing smashed against the half-open driver's side window. Then she began pounding the light steel of the Camry's roof. Snow White swung her bat at Loren's plexiglass windshield again and again till it was a network of spider-web cracks. He sat there petrified, shivering as the stench of fear ran through him. These were the last moments of his life. These furies he'd never seen before were going to force their way into his car and club him to death or into a wheelchair. Over the jackhammer of their assaults he could hear them intoning: "Damnation . . . fire . . . damnation . . . fire . . ." like a ritual incantation. He shrank back in his bucket seat and tasted the acid of panic in his throat.

And then the only sounds were the gentle thunderclaps and the soothing drum of rain. The Kafka nightmare was over. He heard two car doors open and slam shut, a motor purr into life. Highway beams stabbed out across the opposite shoulder and the hags and their attack car vanished again into the storm, back the way they had come. "What what what . . ." he kept mumbling like a helpless child.

How much time passed he could never have said. Then a tractor trailer whooshed through the overpass at sixty or higher and left Loren and the Camry rocking in its wake. The motion forced him back to reality. He made himself slide across to the undamaged passenger side door and open it and emerge into the tunnel like a toad from its hole. Another pair of headlight beams stabbed at him and he stumbled out into the road with his arms waving. A red minivan slued around him in a frantic semicircle into the wrong lane and raced out into the storm. He cursed himself for not having bought the cell phone he'd decided he needed in his car for emergencies.

Turning back to the Camry he stared moronically at its dented roof and hood and shattered windshield. Suddenly he remembered. *I don't have a cell phone but there's a Wisconsin map in my door pocket.* If it wasn't too far to the next town he might risk kicking out the windshield, driving drenched a few miles through the storm. If the Camry could move at all.

Another set of headlight beams came at him along the highway, above them whirling light that shone blue in the inky morning. He staggered into the opposite lane and leapt in the air like a lunatic and this time the car skidded to a stop and a barrel-chested man in the uniform of the Wisconsin State Police stepped out and advanced on Loren with his sidearm aimed at him.

"Two old ladies from nowhere assaulting an automobile with baseball bats. Never heard of such goings on around here before." The trooper closed his notebook and dropped it in the side pocket of his uniform coat. "With no better description of their car except it was big and dark, and the Interstate twenty miles down the road . . . well, I'll give it to you straight, Mr. Mensing, they won't be found unless a miracle happens."

"I felt so . . ." Loren groped for the word he wanted. "Helpless. Powerless. Violated."

"You felt like my sister in Chicago felt when she was raped," the trooper said. "Only you weren't touched. Shouldn't take you long to be yourself again."

"I'll be okay." Two valiums from the toiletries case on the Camry's back seat, washed down with a diet cola from the police cruiser's trunk, had helped ease the sense of dread. But he knew that neither he nor the Camry could make it the rest of the way to Dennison. He turned away from the trooper and watched the pony-tailed beanpole with MOXLEY'S AUTO

REPAIR stitched above the breast pocket of his coveralls finish hoisting the Camry's front end onto the tow truck's winch. "Ready when you are, mister," the beanpole said. Loren waved goodbye to the trooper and climbed into the cab's passenger seat.

The nearest town with an auto repair shop was fourteen miles along the state road. But the storm had vanished, the last thunderheads scudding out of sight to the east, and the wails and bleats from the country music cassette the beanpole had popped into its slot as soon as they'd hit the road were endurable for the twenty minutes before the tow truck turned off the highway at an exit ramp marked VALE POP. 1402. Moxley's Auto Repair was just beyond the interchange. Loren saw an outdoor pay phone near the gas pumps and jumped down from the truck cab as soon as the beanpole had parked.

"That's right," he told the voice that represented his long distance service. "Loren Mensing calling Ms. Heather Dennison. Person to person." While the call was going through he looked at his watch. Not quite eleven. Ninety minutes ago he hadn't even run into the storm. Now the sky was so pure and blue it was hard to believe any of it had happened.

"Dennison residence." A quivery female voice in his ear. For a frantic moment Loren was sure it belonged to one of the old women with the baseball bats. *No way,* the shreds of common sense told him. They couldn't have driven all the way to Dennison in the time since the attack, and besides they'd headed off in the opposite direction, towards the state line. He heard the long distance operator ask for Heather Dennison. "Just a moment, please," the quivery voice said. It was more like five minutes before Loren heard the shy high-pitched voice of the woman who had brought him to the dairy country of Wisconsin.

11

"Heather, it's me," he said. "There's a problem." He told her about the storm and the assault on his car under the overpass.

"Oh God," she said softly. "Oh no." Then: "You're sure you heard them right? Fire and damnation?"

"That's what it sounded like, only I think it was damnation and fire. I may have missed some of it."

She was silent for a few beats too long. "Oh, how awful," she said then.

"The mechanic says they won't have my car ready till Tuesday afternoon," Loren told her. "I'm thinking seriously about turning around and going home."

"Oh, please don't," she said with a desperation in her voice that he didn't think was faked. "Please, I need you so badly. Something—well, something happened to me a few days ago."

"What?" he demanded.

"Look, I can come get you, it's only eighty miles or so, I can be there by twelve thirty and I've already made a reservation for you at the hotel and the concert and cocktail party are this afternoon and . . . You said Moxley's Auto Repair in Vale? Loren, please let's keep going with this." Loren said nothing. "It's so important to so many people who may die if . . ."

All life is risk. What was waiting for him back home but more loneliness? "All right," he cut in. "I'll stay till Tuesday anyway, then you'll have to drive me back here so I can pick up my car. I may decide to go home then."

"I'll see you around twelve thirty," she promised. "Thanks forever."

Disconnected from her, he suddenly realized that he'd had nothing to eat since the bite of stale pastry that along with imitation orange juice and coffee brewed from dishwater had made up the deluxe continental breakfast at the chain motel where he'd spent Saturday night. He opened the door to the auto repair bay and found the beanpole sitting on the oil-smeared concrete floor, contemplating a pickup truck balanced three feet in the air on a rack. "Excuse me," he said. "Is there a place I can get a decent meal around here?"

"Sure is," the mechanic drawled. "Best place in fifty miles is Aunt Emily's Kountry Korner, that's with two K's. Walk down to the traffic light, go left two blocks on Main and you're there. It's in the middle of the block. I've et there twenty years and I still can't figure why she named it the Korner. You want my advice, order the Sunday special."

Ten minutes' walk through the all but empty town and he found the place. The Sunday special proved to be a large orange juice, real this time, and a gargantuan buckwheat cake topped with a fried egg and a sausage patty, home fries on the side, and a bottomless carafe of coffee. It was the unhealthiest meal he'd eaten in years and it made him feel whole again. He lingered over the coffee till twelve-fifteen, then strolled back to the edge of town. A blue Volvo that hadn't been there before was parked at the border of the auto repair lot. As he approached, the driver's side door opened and a woman maneuvered herself out awkwardly. She reached into the car's interior for something Loren couldn't make out until she started hobbling toward him and he saw it was a thick black cane. As he broke into a trot and came up to her he felt the fear rising in him again. They flung their arms around each other.

"What happened to you?" he demanded. "Why on earth didn't you stay in the car?"

"I'm all right," she said. "My knee's sore but I've lived with worse."

"You took a fall or . . . ?"

"I fell after someone with a crowbar or tire iron whacked my kneecap Tuesday night." She winced as Loren brushed against her left leg and tried to smile through the pain. "Charter member of the Tonya Harding fan club I guess. I'll tell you about it on the way in. The doctor says I'll need the cane awhile but there's no permanent damage."

Loren took two steps back and inspected her, the softly curling hair so light brown it was almost dark blonde, the attractive but starved-looking body, those pale blue eyes that seemed to have known a lifetime of suffering but could still gleam now and then with mischievous delight. "Let me drive us back," he said.

"No need. This car has cruise control, I hardly need to use my feet at all." She smiled again. "I guess you'd better get your bags and toss them in the trunk yourself though."

A perfect Sunday afternoon in early May, southwest Wisconsin basking under a cloudless sky, contoured fields planted in hay and corn, bluegrass pastures dotted with grazing cows. The Volvo skimmed through the heart of dairy country at a placid 50 miles per hour. Except for the tension eating at Loren and the unanswered questions roiling through his mind he might have made an adjustment to the deep cushioned passenger seat and nodded off.

"Tuesday night I just couldn't get to sleep," Heather told him. "One of the things I wanted to do in Dennison was learn more about the different businesses the family owned. I hadn't seen Nature's Ovens yet and I knew the bakers worked three shifts so I put on some sweats and drove over, it's only five miles from Aunt Lydia's house. I parked in the side lot and went in through the back door the night shift uses. The foreman was very nice, he gave me a tour of the kitchens. I left just a little before midnight and was walking back to my car

14

when this man came at me with a tire iron or crowbar or something, whacked my kneecap, grabbed my purse and ran towards the rear lot where I guess he'd parked. I heard a car start up and race out the other exit a minute later."

"I know you never saw the car but can you describe the man?"

"Not so it would help. Just a rather small man in a black turtleneck and dark jeans and a ski mask. For the first minute or so I was too stunned and shocked to even feel the pain. Then I started screaming. Luckily one of the night bakers was outside the building on a smoke break. He found me and ran back in and called 911. The police found my purse next morning in a roadside trash can a few miles away. Nothing was taken except twenty or thirty dollars I had in my wallet."

"Why didn't you call?" Loren asked. "Why didn't you tell me?"

She kept her eyes on the empty road as she answered. "I was, well, I was afraid you wouldn't come if I did. But I swear, Loren, I never dreamed anyone would go after you too! And I still can't believe . . . I mean how could they have known . . . ?"

"Lots of people knew I was coming today, right?"

"Yes, but not where you lived or whether you'd be driving or flying or what route you'd take if you did drive. I didn't know that myself!"

"You told them I was a law professor and where I teach. Anyone knowing that much could have found me without breaking a sweat."

"Loren, do you seriously believe those old women were following you all day yesterday and this morning?"

"Tell me what else I should believe," he demanded. "You get attacked with a tire iron or crowbar Tuesday, I get it with baseball bats today. Frankly, my dear, I think you have a rela-

15

tive who has it in for both of us."

She was silent for a mile or two of highway bordered by white fences broken by the entrance gates to one dairy farm after another. Loren saw that Heather was chewing her lower lip as if lost in thought. "Professor Mensing," she said after a while, "one of the many skills you taught me at NYU was how to distinguish cases. Do you mind if I make a few distinctions about us?"

"Be my guest," he invited.

"I was attacked by a young or middle-aged man who tried to cripple me. You were targeted by two old women who didn't touch you but just disabled your car. My man didn't open his mouth. Your women kept reciting something about damnation and fire. And remember, I left Aunt Lydia's Tuesday night on impulse. No one knew I'd go out or where I'd go. Loren, there's very little crime in Dennison but the most sensible theory is that I was hit by a sneak thief. Then today you just happened to be hit by a couple of religious nuts."

"There's another theory possible," Loren said. "Your man stalked you for days, waiting his chance. My old ladies stalked me, waiting theirs. Both sets of stalkers sent after us by one of your relatives."

"Oh, that couldn't be! I mean it's so . . ." She frowned, groping for a word that would give form to her disbelief.

"You said it yourself when you first came to me for help," Loren reminded her. "There's a great deal of money at stake here. Greed breeds ghouls. On the other hand, strange coincidences happen every day. Maybe your theory's the right one. I don't know what to believe. Let's give it a rest . . . God, this is lovely country." He surrendered to the warmth and peace of the Sunday afternoon, felt himself drifting off.

What gentled him awake was darkly beautiful string music

from the Volvo's stereo radio. Two violins, a viola, a cello. After a few moments he recognized it as Schubert's magnificent D minor quartet, "Death and the Maiden." He stirred in his seat and Heather took her eyes from the road to smile at him. "That's the Dennison Chamber Ensemble," she said, "live on KDEN. Two more of the family holdings, the ensemble and the station I mean."

"They're playing it superbly," Loren said.

"You'll meet the performers at the reception," she promised. "If you hadn't run into trouble we'd both be in the audience at Dennison Hall."

"What time is it?" Loren blinked behind his glasses, shut his weak left eye and tried to focus with his right on the dashboard clock's readout before he realized he didn't have to. In their last phone conversation before he set out for Wisconsin she'd told him the concert would begin at two, and the musicians were still in Schubert's first movement. "I figure around two-ten. We must be getting close."

"Seven miles to the city line," she said. "Enjoy." Loren closed both eyes and let the music enter him. It was during the *andante con moto* second movement with its dark variations of the death theme from the first that he felt the Volvo swing off the highway. Just beyond the cloverleaf interchange Heather braked under the canopy of a nondescript motel with CHEESE COUNTRY INN in gold leaf over the doorway. "We're here," she told him as if he couldn't have guessed. "It's hours before the reception, you might as well check in now."

"You get to stay in Aunt Lydia's mansion and I get to stay here?" It bothered him. Penny-pinching didn't square with his sense of her.

"Oh, silly, you don't stay *here*," she laughed. "The old motel is for casual travelers. Special guests get the executive wing. It's a separate building three blocks up the street. *Much* nicer. Just sign in and pick up your key and I'll drive you over."

Loren approached the registration counter just inside the Cheese Country Inn's double doors and identified himself to the acne-pitted youth behind the desk. "Oh, yes, sir, Ms. Dennison told me all about you, sir. Welcome to the finest little city in southwest Wisconsin." If he had had a forelock he might have tugged it like a deferential prole in a Victorian novel. "Room 22," he said as he handed Loren a key. "That's the executive wing, second level. The same key lets you into the building and unlocks the breakfast room on the ground floor. Complimentary continental breakfast every morning six to nine, serve yourself, all you care to eat. Bagels, muffins, cold cereal, fruit, yogurt, three kinds of juice, hazelnut coffee regular and decaf. Whoops, almost forgot." He swooped under the counter and emerged a second later with a video-cassette in a plain white cardboard case. "The TV in your room has a built-in video player. Chamber of Commerce had this cassette made last year, it tells visitors all about the area. Runs thirty minutes. No extra charge." He swiveled his turkey neck towards the Volvo outside the double doors. "That's Ms. Dennison with you, sir, isn't it? Thought so. Here." He swooped out of sight for another second and came up with a second key. "Err, just in case you lose the first one," he said as he struggled to keep a smirk out of his voice.

"Thanks," Loren replied inanely and, before the youth might offer him a box of condoms too, he walked swiftly out.

At the third corner beyond the original motel Heather turned right. Halfway down the long block, between two small cornfields and with conventional tract houses across the street, stood an unmarked three-story brick structure with parking slots for perhaps a dozen cars to one side. "Behold the executive wing," Heather proclaimed. "No clerks, no bellhops and on Sundays hardly any guests. A few out-of-towners with business here tomorrow may show up while we're at the reception but you'll probably have most of the building to yourself."

No wonder that kid was thinking X-rated thoughts, Loren told himself. Playfully, just to gauge her reaction, he rubbed the two keys together and offered one to Heather. That impish smile came into her eyes as she took the key from him. "You don't want sex with a cripple," she said.

"I never discriminate against the handicapped," Loren insisted righteously. "Can't. It's illegal."

"Anyway I'll hold onto this for a while." She let the key slide sensuously through her fingers into the mouth of her purse. "Just to keep you interested. Now you go unpack, clean up, take a walk around the neighborhood, whatever. I'll pick you up at quarter to five for the reception."

"You've done enough chauffeuring for one day," he told her. "I'll take a cab. And no offense," he added, dipping into her purse to retrieve the second key, "but I'll take this too. I'd welcome a late night visit from you but what if that hypothetical greedy relative of yours should borrow it and come by to tuck me in?"

Room 22 turned out to be not a room but a spacious suite: rich blue carpet, chintz-covered chairs and couch, tabletops glistening with lemon oil, a small kitchen with microwave, coffee maker and mini refrigerator. Loren showered in the whirlpool tub, found KDEN on the radio beside the king-size bed and napped through most of a piece that sounded like Charles Ives. When he came awake the chamber ensemble was playing the haunting eighth string quartet by Shostakovich but somehow he forced himself to click the radio off. In robe and slippers he padded into the suite's front room, inserted the Chamber of Commerce cassette into the videoplayer-TV combo nestled within an armoire, settled back in a wing chair.

"Welcome to Dennison in the heart of southwest Wisconsin!" boomed a faux-brisk narrator as aerial shots displayed lushly rolling countryside followed by bird's-eye views of downtown. "We're delighted you came to visit. Our community was founded in 1846 by settlers of English, Swiss and German stock who elected Hiram Dennison their first mayor." Shots copied from old daguerrotypes segueing into color video footage of a traditional courthouse. "The red brick courthouse in the heart of downtown was completed in 1891, the year Dennison became our county seat." Consumers in family groups strolling the downtown streets. "Our historic business district features dozens of quaint small shops. As you make your way around the Square you imagine you've traveled back in time a hundred years to when local farmers sold their produce from the backs of horse-drawn wagons." Archival footage of the town, dating from the infancy of the moving image, followed by slick commercial shots of photogenic young men and women at play. "The Dennison area offers endless opportunities for recreation. Whether you hike, bike, golf, swim, fish, sail or do cross country skiing, we have it all for you."

Smooth tracking shots of well-groomed suburban houses, gardens, manicured lawns. "A drive through our neighborhoods will show you that the friendly Norman Rockwell hometown feeling is alive and well in Dennison." Cut to black-and-white newsreel footage of a dignified man in middle age who vaguely reminded Loren of the actor Walter Huston, strolling along a spacious avenue with walking stick in hand, wearing a lightweight suit and tie and fedora and spats. "Our economy is strong and prosperous, thanks largely to the courage and vision of Almon Dennison, grandson of our founder, who revitalized this area in the worst years of the depression, risking his own fortune and going deeply into debt for the sake of his neighbors and his town, bringing master craftsmen over from Europe to develop the area's dairy industries, creating new businesses when old ones were dying every day." Modern color footage of brick-shaped yellow slabs coasting along conveyor belts. "Visit the Alpendenn plant, founded by Almon Dennison in 1933, and watch the making of your favorite cheeses, Swiss, Gruyere, Muenster, natural smoked cheddar, then drop in at the adjoining outlet store and purchase all you want. Enjoy a fine lunch in Alpendenn's dining room." Cut to shots of a huge bakery kitchen. "Visit nationally famous Nature's Ovens and enjoy the delicious aromas of the most healthful breads in America, millet, cracked wheat, German rye, seven grain herb bread, rolls, muffins, biscuits. Nature's Ovens loaves are baked in a custom-designed slow-baking hearth oven, three thousand loaves every hour, 24 hours a day, for shipment throughout this wonderful land of ours. There's an outlet store on the premises too—with free samples!" The narrator didn't say so but Loren knew from Heather that Nature's Ovens was a Dennison family enterprise too. It was in the bakery parking lot that her knee had been whacked.

"Thousands come to Dennison every year in summer for the annual Cheese Days, Bread Days and Dairy Days celebrations," the booster voice went on as the TV screen showed crowds of tourists, fireworks, game booths, a ferris wheel. Then some sedate shots, a colonnaded building with DENNISON HALL on brass plaques at each side of its entrance doors, four tuxedoed musicians performing before a

21

packed house. "Thanks to the tireless efforts of Lydia Dennison, widow of Almon and our prime civic bene-factor"—cut to an elegantly gowned frosted-haired woman Loren guessed to be in her late fifties, standing at a micro-phone on the concert stage—"we are visited year round by lovers of great music who come to hear the Dennison Chamber Ensemble, or visiting groups like the Amadeus Quartet who have made our community a regular stop on their tours. All our chamber concerts are broadcast live on KDEN, which is owned by the Dennison Cultural Founda-tion and has been voted one of America's outstanding clas-sical FM stations." At the video's end the director reprised the opening aerial shot but this time moving from downtown outward to the Edenic countryside. "So welcome to Dennison in the heart of southwest Wisconsin! Relax, enjoy —and don't forget to come back!"

Loren rose and pressed the Rewind button. He wasn't sur-prised that the infomercial said nothing about Almon Dennison's strange will, the testament which had brought his grandniece to Loren and Loren in turn to this town. No chamber of commerce in its right mind would have breathed a word of it.

Freshly shaved and decked out in the pinstripes he usually reserved for oral argument in appellate courts, Loren thumbed through the yellow pages of the Dennison phone directory in his night-table drawer and, with no basis for a reasoned choice, punched out the number of the company at the top of the list. "Call Me a Taxi," said a cheerful black woman's voice.

"Okay, you're a taxi," Loren replied automatically, and felt his ears burn.

"We just *got* to change that company name," the woman

sighed, then switched to a flat impersonal tone. "Do you require cab service, sir?"

"Yes, please. My name is Mensing and I'm staying at the Cheese Country Inn, executive wing. I want to go to Mrs. Lydia Dennison's house. I'm afraid I don't know the address."

"Everyone around here knows that address," the woman chuckled. "Your cab will be in front of the executive wing in ten minutes."

"So will I," Loren promised. "Thanks very much."

When he stepped out of the building a vintage Ford station wagon, painted burgundy and with CALL ME A TAXI and the company's phone number in neat white lettering on both rear doors, was waiting for him with the motor idling. Loren opened one of the doors and climbed in. The driver was a black man with close-cropped gray hair and mustache. "Miss Lydia's place you said, right?"

"Right." Loren glanced at his watch and found it was almost five. He wondered if being fashionably late was acceptable in Dennison. The driver made two lefts, swooped past the main motel where Loren had checked in, followed the cloverleaf interchange to a connecting road.

"This your first visit here, sir?" They were on another two-lane blacktop, amid gently rolling hills where cows were grazing. In the far distance Loren could make out a stately white house he guessed was his destination, dominating the countryside from atop the highest hill in sight.

"Yes, it is. I caught your promotional video this afternoon. Seems like a nice place to live."

"Oh, it is indeed that. Specially if you like cheese and . . ." He paused as if groping for the words he wanted. "And chamber music. That's what this town mostly runs on, cheese

23

and chamber music. You know Miss Lydia, sir?"

"I'll be meeting her for the first time in a few minutes," Loren said.

"She's some fine lady. Must be eighty at least and she look not much older than yourself. Without her and her husband before her, why this whole county'd be a dried-up little hole now. You admire this chamber music, sir?"

"Yes," Loren admitted. "Very much."

"Then you come to the right place. People go to Memphis for jazz, they go to Kentucky for bourbon. When they want chamber music they come here. That's all her doing. Miss Lydia's. The money she sunk into making us a music place! Why, the folks that make their living playing that stuff, they all work for her. Least for that Cultural Foundation her husband set up in his will. Just like the people at Nature's Ovens and the Alpendenn cheese folks work for other companies her family owns." He swerved off the blacktop onto a dirt road that wound around the hill at whose peak the mansion stood. As the cab passed under a gray stone archway the road widened dramatically, sweeping towards the house and gardens. Dozens of cars were angle parked on the grass at the road's edge. Absently scanning their rear license plates, Loren noticed something he'd never encountered before. MOZART. MAHLER. EROICA. JSBACH. Half the people at this reception seemed to have come in cars with the names of classical composers or compositions on their plates.

"Excuse me," Loren said. "Am I seeing things, or . . . ?"

"Just seeing what out there," the driver told him. "Few years ago Miss Lydia dreamed up this plan to hook more folks on her kind of music. Anyone wanted vanity license plates with one of those names on them, she'd foot the bill. Her business manager made a deal with the state for a cut rate but part of the deal was every plate had to have six letters or numbers, no more, no less. Saved money making 'em that way I guess. Now that ain't my kind of music but I hear a lot of those classical cats had names with a bunch more than six letters, so some of the folks took her up on her offer had to be kinda creative about it."

"I don't suppose you were one of them?"

"Well, yes and no." The cab slid to a halt in front of white-painted pillars three stories high. "You see, I don't push and I don't shove but I ain't a shy man neither. I happened to see Miss Lydia downtown one day and I introduced myself and said: 'Ma'am, I'd sure love to have a set of those license plates for my cab but you know there just ain't no black guys *wrote* that kind of music.' And she agreed with me right away. Said I could use one of my own favorite music folks long as the name had just six letters. Which meant I had to be kinda creative too." He beamed ecstatically as Loren handed him a ten across the back of the front seat. "Thank *you*, sir," he said, and reached into a dashboard cubbyhole for a business card which he handed back. "You need a ride when the party's over, you just call you a taxi."

As the station wagon U-turned and headed down the hill, Loren caught the name on its rear plate.

SACHMO.

An ancient maid in dark dress and white apron answered his ring. "Come this way, sir," she said, and Loren recognized the quivery voice that had answered the phone here this morning. She led him down a broad oak-paneled hall, weaving around clusters of chattering guests with wine glasses in their hands and tuxedoed servers proffering trays of hot hors-d'oeuvres. Beyond a majestic staircase blocked off with red velvet rope, the open double doors of what Loren took to be a ballroom revealed something like two hundred men and women roaming about, sipping, nibbling, their small talk generating a noise level like artillery. Loren cast longing looks at the portable bars that dotted the room as he followed the maid through the mob towards an alcove with a bay window. Heather sat in one of the four brocaded armchairs, her cane's curved handle crooked over the chair's back, a plate of snacks on the low table beside her. Loren bent to kiss her, then turned to the next chair, on whose edge sat the frosted-haired woman he'd seen in the video less than an hour before.

"Mrs. Dennison," he said, offering his hand, "I'm Loren Mensing. Sorry I'm a little late."

"It's a pleasure to meet you at last. Heather's told me so much about you, what a brilliant teacher you are and, well, everything. Welcome to Dennison."

She was a classic beauty, her body as firm as that of any other woman in the room, the verve and poise of an athlete in her movements, the skill of an actress in the modulations of her voice. Could she really be almost eighty? There were amazingly few lines around her eyes but he noticed that above her white silk blouse and long dark skirt she wore a blue scarf as if to hide what the years had done to her neck. She rose with a dancer's grace and took Loren's hand in her cool assured grip. "Let me introduce you around," she said, and escorted him to the other chairs in the alcove.

"Professor Mensing, Miles Lewis." A wispy old man in a navy blazer who by his looks might have been Lydia's father. "Miles was one of my husband's right-hand men when Almon turned this town around back in the Thirties. He's also the last of Almon's associates who's still alive." Lewis bobbed his head affably but didn't stir, and Loren wondered if he'd heard a word. Lydia lost no time moving on to the fourth chair. "Professor Mensing, my grandnephew Clay

Brean." A round-faced jowly man perhaps forty, encased in a suit that fit him like a sausage skin, an obvious toupee of auburn shade on his dome, a plate heaped with crab Rangoon in his ample lap. *The first of the relatives I get to meet,* Loren thought as he extended his hand. But obviously not the one who'd attacked Heather in the parking lot. That man she'd described as rather small.

Lydia steered Loren in the direction of three men in business suits and a grave-faced young woman, standing in a loose group just outside the alcove. The woman wore a floor-length black dress and her eyes blinked behind gold-framed spectacles. "Professor Mensing, I'd like you to meet Ellis Carr, the program director at KDEN . . . Ralph Wolfe, our mayor . . . Dan Feinberg who manages the Dennison Cultural Foundation . . . and this is Ellis' wife, Manya Wentz, principal cellist of the Chamber Ensemble. If you had come in time for the concert you could have heard her playing 'Death and the Maiden.' "

"I did catch part of it on KDEN," Loren said, and looked into her strangely blinking eyes as he took her offered hand. "I've never heard it played better."

The only one of the four who seemed curious about Loren was Feinberg, a tall cadaverous man with burning dark eyes who gave the impression of an intellectual who never slept. He kept the fingers of his left hand twined around a cold pipe as if he wished he dared light up. "And what brings you to Dennison, Professor?" he asked.

"Oh, Dan, I'm sorry, I guess the news missed you somehow." Heather pushed out of her chair, reached for her cane, came over to put her arm in Loren's and lean intimately against him. "Dan, and any of the rest of you who haven't heard," she announced, "this is the man I love. We're going to be married next month."

Loren held her close and tried to summon up a skill he'd been compelled to master as a young associate in his father's law firm before he'd broken away to academic life: the ability to keep a supportive face during courtroom or deposition testimony by the firm's clients that Loren knew the clients knew was false. He sorely needed that skill now.

Because the truth was that he hardly knew Heather Dennison at all.

TWO

He had seen her four hours a week for more than three months and she meant only a face in a sea of faces, a name on a printout junked at semester's end. During the fall of the 1986–87 academic year when Loren had been a visiting professor at New York University School of Law, Heather Dennison had been one of the ninety-odd students who had taken his course in Decedents' Estates and Trusts. Or so she claimed when she called him almost eight years later at the Midwest law school that was his base. "I'm sure you don't remember me," she said. "I never contributed much in class unless the professor bullied me and you weren't the bullying type."

"I'm sorry," he said into the phone. "I'm getting so old I can hardly remember the names of people who've been on the faculty with me for twenty years. I'll take your word for it you were in my class at NYU. Are you practicing in New York now?"

"I dropped out of law school right after the semester I had you. It took a year and a half to realize being a lawyer wasn't for me. I—well, some friends and I run a shelter for abused women and children."

She's going to hit me for a contribution, Loren thought. "You helped," she went on. "Some of the things you said in class . . . I caught on that being a lawyer means being completely amoral and I don't think I am so I left."

"Good for you," he said.

"Although I never could figure out why you kept on being a law professor. Teaching people how to be amoral for fun and profit. Because I don't think you are either."

Loren could have told her but she was only a phone voice he might never have heard before. The empty nights courting sleep with liquor and valium, reciting to himself the endless lullaby *I train whores*. "So what can I do for you?" he asked coolly.

"I want to make an appointment to fly out and see you," she said. "My hours at the shelter are flexible, any day that's good for you is fine with me. I have, well, sort of a legal problem. Big one."

"One you think I can help you with?"

"One you actually taught us about at NYU. In general anyway. Remember how you spent like two hours on restrictions in wills and trusts that were based on beneficiaries' religion or lifestyle or who they married?"

That was when he knew she had really been one of his students. "I still give that pitch every time I teach Estates and Trusts," he said.

"Are you teaching it this semester?"

"No."

"Then you might want to review your notes," she said.

They were to meet at his law school office at four on a Thursday afternoon a few weeks before the end of the academic year. That semester his Thursday classes were over at two. When he returned to the office a few minutes after the hour he found a message from her on his voice mail: her plane had landed on time, she was staying at the Auberge, she was looking forward to seeing him soon. Loren knew the Auberge was a small European-style hotel at the edge of the city, not grossly expensive but no Motel 6 either. The choice suggested she wasn't poor.

He killed time leafing through law journal articles, going over his class notes on the types of restrictions in trusts that she'd mentioned, straightening the chaos of books and papers in which he worked. The clock radio on his credenza read 3:58 when a soft tap sounded on his door. "Come in," he called.

She stood framed in the doorway for a moment as if she were posing for him and he still didn't recognize her. Her self-description over the phone had been good: five-ten, painfully thin, long curly hair poised between blonde and brunette. With a slender tawny briefcase clutched beside the shoulder bag under her left arm she stepped in and came toward him. "I'm Heather Dennison," she said. "I really appreciate your seeing me. Do I call you Loren or Professor Mensing or what?"

"Loren's fine." She'd said over the phone that the years in New York had not robbed her of the accent of Wisconsin where she'd been raised: right again. "Sit down." He gestured towards the dark red leather couch which for once was not cluttered with law books. She sat back in the cushions and carefully studied his face.

"I guess we both look a little older," she said.

"Well, I'm over fifty now. Full-fledged member of AARP. And I've had a few medical adventures since I was at NYU."

"Oh, no," she said softly. "Not anything serious?"

"My left eye's worse and I had an angioplasty a few years ago. I need to take an aspirin and a Cardizem tablet every morning for the rest of my life." If she had dropped out of law school after the fall 1986 semester she wouldn't know about the emotional horrors that had scarred him a few months later. None of her business anyway.

"You must have to watch what you eat then," she said.

"Most of the time I'm pretty careful. I eat much less meat than I used to and it's usually broiled chicken or fish. Is there a reason why it matters?"

"Well, I've been told the dining room at the Auberge is one of the Midwest's best kept culinary secrets," she said, "and I'd like to take you to dinner tonight. If you're free?"

"I'm free every night," he replied tonelessly, and glanced at the credenza against his office wall. "But there's plenty of time to talk over your problem before we go. If I need to do legal research, here we are."

She crossed her right knee over her left and leaned forward, her pale blue eyes bright with remembrance. "Back at NYU when you began talking about trusts," she said, "you polled us. Asked if any of us were actually beneficiaries of a trust."

He nodded and waited for her to continue.

"I didn't raise my hand then," she confessed, "but I'm one of those. Ever since I was born I've gotten several thousand dollars a year from the estate of my great-uncle, Almon Dennison. Does that name mean anything to you?"

When he admitted he'd never heard it before she gave a thumbnail sketch of the life of the man who more or less at Loren's age had gambled his inherited wealth and borrowed millions more in a desperate effort to restore prosperity to the Depression-wracked Wisconsin community his grandfather had helped found in 1846. "When Uncle Almon died," she finished, "he was 86 years old and worth five times what he'd been worth in the Thirties. He died in 1964, a while before I was born."

"He never knew you but left you enough so you'd never have to work," Loren remarked. "Lucky lady."

"Oh, he didn't leave it to me *personally!* It was a trust fund.

32

Except for charitable bequests his will left almost everything he owned in trust. His widow, my great-aunt Lydia—she was forty years younger and she's still healthy as a horse and one of the most vital people I know—well, half the income from the trust goes to Lydia as long as she lives and she has a testamentary general power of appointment over half the corpus."

The jargon rolled trippingly off her tongue as if she'd taken his course this year. Not only did Lydia Dennison enjoy half the income from what was obviously a huge fund but in her own will she could direct the disposition of half the principal. Another very lucky lady, Loren reflected. "How about the other half?" he asked.

Heather lifted the slender briefcase to her lap, zipped it open and took out a manila folder from which she removed a single long sheet of paper with perforations permitting it to be folded accordion-wise. Then she motioned Loren to sit on the couch beside her. "I made this copy for you," she said. "It's the Dennison family tree going back to Hiram's generation, and Hiram fought in Andrew Jackson's troop at the battle of New Orleans. When Uncle Almon died, the attorneys hired a genealogist to prepare this and it's been updated every two years since. It's on computer disk now of course."

"I assume most of this isn't relevant to the trust?"

"More than you might think," she told him, and folded the document along its perforations so that Almon Dennison's generation and the one before him were uppermost. "Uncle Almon never had any children," she said, touching the square that contained his name with a short unpolished fingernail. "But you can see he had three brothers and two sisters—he outlived all of them—and his father and mother had seven siblings between them. His nearest blood relatives when he died were nephews, nieces and distant cousins."

Loren took the document from her lap, studied it for a

minute, then refolded it until the present generation was uppermost. Heather, he saw, was the daughter of one of Almon's nephews. She was an only child and both her parents were dead.

"You asked about the other half." Heather extracted from her briefcase a photocopied document at least two inches thick. "This is a copy of Uncle Almon's will I brought for you. It says the income from the other half of the trust property is to be split equally among the issue of his father's and mother's siblings and of his own siblings who are alive at the time of his death."

"Wait a minute." Loren took the will from her and set it on his lap with the family tree. "Didn't you tell me a few minutes ago that Almon died before you were born? Then how could you be . . . Ah, of course. Your mother must have been pregnant with you before Almon's death."

"Exactly," she said. "I was born five months later. The trust company had to go to court and get an order declaring that I was a member of the beneficiary class. There were twenty-three of us originally. I'm the youngest."

"And as the older members of the class die off, the survivors' shares keep getting bigger?"

"Ahh—yeah," she muttered, and looked down at her hands as if she were embarrassed or ashamed at the colossal luck that had been her birth gift.

"Mind telling me how much your share is now?"

She bit down on her lower lip before she answered. "Around sixty thousand a year," she said, then added in a tone Loren took to be self-defensive: "It used to be a lot less." But of course she must have been receiving some money every year literally since she was born. A guardianship account would have been set up for her share until she became an adult. *Nice deal if you can get it,* he thought ruefully.

Then something else struck him, perhaps a flash of lawyerly intuition.

"How long does this arrangement go on?" he asked. "When does the trust terminate?"

"When Aunt Lydia dies," she said.

"And what happens to the principal then?"

"Well, as I told you before, half of it goes wherever her will says it goes. The other half is split among those who are income beneficiaries at the time of her death."

Loren did some rapid mental arithmetic. If the trust made ten percent a year after expenses, Heather's share of the principal today would run around six hundred thousand dollars. If the trust earned a more realistic five percent, her share of the principal would approach a million and a quarter. To a nonspecialist the testamentary trust on Loren's lap would have been gibberish but to a lawyer versed in the field it seemed straightforward enough. *If it's really that simple,* he asked himself, *why is she here with me?*

Groping under the will for the copy of the Dennison family tree, he noticed checkmarks in red ink next to Heather's name and those of seven others near the foot of the document. Beside each of a larger number of names from the same and earlier generations was a neat little X in the same red ink. "Am I reading these notations right?" He handed the perforated paper across the couch to Heather. "You and these other seven people are the only income beneficiaries left?"

"That's, that's right." Self-defensive mumble again. Loren began counting the X marks on the document. Nine, ten, eleven . . . fifteen in all, which when added to the eight survivors made twenty-three.

"These fifteen are the beneficiaries who've died since you were born," he said.

She chewed her lower lip savagely and with something like guilt in her eyes she nodded. *I wonder if they all died of natural causes,* Loren said to himself, while aloud he changed the subject.

"Okay," he asked, "where's the restriction in the trust? What do you have to do if you want to stay a beneficiary? Believe in Almon's religion? Never smoke or drink?"

"Paragraph 39K," she said, so softly he could hardly make out the words. "See for yourself." He flipped through the pages of the will in his lap and stopped at one she had dog-eared in advance.

" 'Thirty-nine K,' " he read aloud. " '(1) My trustees are hereby directed to cease all payment of income forthwith to any beneficiary under this trust who is not lawfully married by the time of said beneficiary's thirtieth birthday. (2) My trustees are further directed that no person removed as an income beneficiary pursuant to this provision shall receive any share in the principal of this trust upon the termination thereof.' " He squeezed his eyes shut and performed more mental arithmetic. If Heather was a second year student at NYU in the fall of 1986, today she'd probably be . . . "When do you turn thirty?" he asked abruptly.

"December fifth," she shot back.

"And I take it you're not married." It wasn't a question. Her fingers were without rings, but more important, if she had a husband she wouldn't need Loren.

"No," she told him, "and I don't want to be."

"But if you're not married within the next eight months, you get cut out of the trust."

"Unless," she said, "you find a hole in the trust for me to crawl through."

The Auberge was a three-story structure of brick stained

dark red, tucked away on a side street near the city limits amid modernistic buildings that housed investment brokers and HMOs. At six the soft-lit paneled dining room was empty except for a few old couples mechanically munching the early bird special and a sprinkling of drinkers on stools at the bar. "They tell me business picks up later," Heather whispered to Loren as a waiter in white shirt, bow tie and earring led them to a corner table far from other customers. Goblets of ice water, a crock of soft cheddar and a basket of melba toast were arrayed on the white linen cloth. Heather ordered a diet cola and Loren bourbon on rocks. "If it won't bother you? My doctor advised me to have two drinks a night. Good for my heart." He didn't mention the empty evenings when he didn't stop with two.

"I don't mind other people drinking," she said. "But if I ever started using it . . . It would be so easy to get a bottle and shut out the horrors I see every day at the shelter but I'm afraid if I started I couldn't stop and then what use would I be to those women and kids?"

"I can't even interest you in wine to go with dinner?"

"Well," she conceded with a shy smile, "the shelter's a long way off tonight."

Over the cheddar and bowls of turtle soup with a cruet of sherry on the side, their talk drifted back to Almon Dennison's trust. "I can't recall a restriction like his," Loren said. "But I've heard of some weird ones. Remember the one I mentioned in class about the Englishman who left money to a church provided they scheduled all their services to the true time of the sun?"

"Like it was yesterday," she said, stirring sherry into her soup. "And the man who left part of a trust fund to a relative named Thaddeus J. Boyd provided for the rest of his life he signed his name T. Jackson Boyd. God, people are crazy . . ."

You know, most of us who signed up for your course thought Estates and Trusts would be a yawner but you made it—well, come alive."

Loren was afraid he'd blush if the conversation kept on this track. "Let's see how much you remember," he said. "What's the basic principle that governs restrictions in wills and trusts?"

"What you used to call the fundamental one-liner," she answered without hesitation. "It was the testator's property when he was alive so in general he can leave it as he pleases after he's dead. Of course there are exceptions like the forced share for a surviving spouse but that's the general rule."

"Suppose he leaves his property in trust," Loren asked, "but provides that a beneficiary will be cut out if he does or doesn't do certain things?"

"The restriction is valid unless it's illegal, impossible to perform, too vague for a court to figure what it means, or against public policy."

"Did you get an A in my exam?"

"Just a B," she admitted. "I was pretty sure by then that I didn't want to stay in law school so I didn't study hard. But I went over my old class notes before I flew out here."

The waiter whisked away their soup bowls and set a platter with salmon filet and a baked potato in front of Loren, pasta con broccoli before Heather. In the center of the table he deposited a half bottle of Chardonnay. "This is a place worth coming back to," Loren said after sampling the fish. "Where were we? Oh yes, I was telling you that I've run across lots of strange restrictions in trusts. In most of them the dead person's trying to use money like a carrot or a club, to control beneficiaries' religious beliefs or whom they marry or how they raise their children. Your great-uncle broke the mold. He didn't say you had to marry a Christian or you couldn't marry a Jew or an Asian, he just said you had to marry by the time you were thirty. I don't understand that. It doesn't seem to be racial or religious bigotry. Was the man a control freak on principle?"

"Oh, that's right, I didn't tell you the family secret." Heather toyed with her pasta but left most of it uneaten. "Two of Almon's father's brothers turned out to be closet homosexuals. So did one of his own brothers. And he had a sister who never married, never dated men and lived with another woman all her adult life. This was long before gay liberation of course. Almon was terrified that a strain of, well, he'd have called it sexual perversion ran in the family. He thought he could frustrate any other latent homosexuals he was related to by bribing them."

"For a tycoon he was remarkably stupid in some ways," Loren said.

"Aren't we all? But of course very few people knew much about homosexuality back when he made his will."

"And legally its dumbness doesn't mean a thing," Loren pointed out. "If it's not illegal, unclear, impossible to comply with or against public policy, it stands."

"I know that's what you taught us," she said, "but it's insane! Don't I have a constitutional right to decide for myself if I want to get married or not?"

"There can't be a violation of a constitutional right unless there's government action. Almon Dennison wasn't government."

"But that restriction is a worthless sheet of paper unless the courts will enforce it. And the Supreme Court . . . Didn't the Court hold it was unconstitutional for courts to enforce those old deeds that had clauses saying you could never sell the land to a black person?"

"*Shelley v. Kraemer,* 1948," replied Loren, who also

taught constitutional law. "But that was a race-based restriction in a property deed. We're talking about, well, I guess you'd call it a lifestyle-based restriction in a trust. No court has ever extended *Shelley* that far."

"And I can't claim the restriction's too vague," she said, then paused for a forkful of pasta. "And I suppose I can't say it's impossible to comply with." Loren sensed she had some doubt about the latter proposition. "How about general public policy apart from the Constitution? You know, individual autonomy as the ultimate American value, all that law professor stuff?"

"This is the land of the fundamental one-liner," Loren said. "Property is king. Property trumps autonomy. I could argue your theory for you in court but I'd never bet a cent we'd win."

"So what then?" The waiter cleared away the plates and the empty wine bottle and brought a wedge of pecan pie, two dessert plates and forks, a pot of decaf. "Do you see any other possibilities?"

Loren split the pie and filled their cups. "Maybe one," he said. "But to know if it's viable I have to ask you a very personal question." He waited for her to signal that he could ask it but she kept her face blank.

"You have a marvelous command of language," she said at last. "I'll bet you can tell me what you have in mind without invading my privacy."

He thought about it through a bite of pie and a swallow of coffee. "All right, let's assume that one of the beneficiaries under this trust—not you, one of the other women — is a lesbian. If she were living openly with another woman the way Almon's sister was, and if she were getting near thirty and didn't want to lose her trust money, I think I'd advise her to relocate to Hawaii with her partner, find a minister in the gay rights movement and get married now."

"Hawaii?" She frowned as if he'd suggested a move to the heart of darkness.

"*Baehr v. Lewin,*" Loren explained. From the puzzled look that came over her Loren was certain she'd never heard of the case. "You do remember the Equal Rights Amendment? The one that never became part of the U.S. Constitution because not enough states ratified it?"

"Any woman who ever spent a day in law school knows about the ERA."

"Well, there's a provision in the Hawaii state constitution that's almost identical to the ERA. The Hawaii Supreme Court ruled last year that the state law requiring marriage partners to be of opposite sexes presumptively violated that provision."

"Oh," she said blankly.

"The case isn't over yet," Loren went on. "There was a remand for argument on whether the law is narrowly tailored and justified by compelling state interests. If the court sticks to its position the next time around, it will mean that two women in Hawaii can be what Almon's trust describes as 'lawfully married.' However that case turns out, going through a marriage ceremony in Hawaii now would give your hypothetical relative a halfway plausible legal basis for arguing she's complied with the restriction and can't be cut out of the trust." Heather's face still showed no expression. "Have I helped you any?" Loren ventured.

"Nice try," she replied, "but I'm afraid not. There's no woman in my life I'd want to marry."

"And your principles won't let you go through a meaningless ritual with a man friend just for the money?"

"If—well, if nothing else works I'm just not sure what I'll do. Loren, it's not for myself. All the money I ever took from the trust I've put into the shelter. There are so many women and children whose lives are unimaginable nightmares." Her voice dropped to a hoarse whisper. "They're—sort of like the Jews in Hitler's death camps and I'm Schindler with his list. All I can save is a handful. But I will save that handful! I *have* to stay in the trust for their sake." Loren was riveted by the intensity that suddenly seemed to surround her like an aura, and wondered if this was how listeners felt when they heard Joan of Arc.

"This is getting too personal," she said, and half rose in her chair to signal the waiter for the check. "I need you to come up to my room with me. Please don't get the wrong idea."

"The wrong idea," Loren told her, feeling clammy sweat trickle down his spine, "is the furthest thing from my mind."

It was an elegant room, dominated by a queen-size bed he fought to keep from staring at as Heather led him across to a pair of upholstered club chairs facing the window that overlooked the dark street. A few workaholic investment brokers left the office building opposite the Auberge, trudging towards their cars. "So," Loren asked her, "what revelations are too intimate for downstairs?"

"Someone is trying to kill me. He's out there stalking me now." She said it with professional composure like a cancer specialist announcing that a tumor was malignant but Loren could feel the terror beneath the calm. "What I saw you were thinking awhile ago—that one of the beneficiaries has been getting richer over the years by killing off others—I'm certain that's true. And I'm next."

Paranoia, Loren thought, until a more complex theory took its place. As a teen-ager, too young to understand what death meant, how many times might she have wished for another Dennison beneficiary to die so that she might enjoy more consumer goods? The guilt she felt as an adult at the rise in her own net worth because of others dying was so thick he could almost touch it. Might she not be projecting some of that guilt onto an unspecified fellow survivor, fantasizing him or her as a mass murderer? "If that's what you believe," he advised, "you'd better go to the police."

"Loren, I have no facts to back this up. No rational basis. I just *know*."

"No one's threatened you? You haven't had any close calls, accidents that might have been something else?"

"Not the kind you mean." She cut off the sentence so sharply he sensed her fear that she'd given away a secret. "You have to understand," she went on, "at the shelter we get threats from abusive husbands and boyfriends. Back in December someone whispered 'Bitch' into my ear and tried to shove me off a platform at the Chambers Street subway station near the courthouses. It was a miracle I didn't go over onto the third rail. That kind of danger is part of the life I've chosen. I can deal with it. This is different."

"Different how?"

"This is not some primitive brute after me, it's a cold rational person who's made a deliberate choice to kill other human beings. It's like the Nazis. Pure evil."

Loren wondered if perhaps she hadn't seen *Schindler's List* once too often and struggled to keep her mood from creeping over him. "Heather," he said, "I've known too many women to reject intuitive certainties out of hand but couldn't we please light the lamp of reason for a minute? Let's assume *arguendo* that you're partly right. One of the other seven survivors has been killing off relatives over the years as he sees the chance. But don't you see he'd have to be an idiot to go after you now? He must know you're almost thirty and still single. Why would he risk the death penalty to kill you when if he just sits on his ass till December fifth he profits by precisely the same amount?"

"I know," she said. "I've thought of that. All I can come up with is that there's some reason why he feels he has to kill me anyway. But in any case there are others he's killed—remember you're assuming I'm right that far—and I've gained too by those deaths. I have to do something to, well, to atone for that."

This conversation, Loren reflected as he squirmed in his chair, was getting crazier every minute. Trying to preserve the facade of lawyerly analysis, he asked: "Just what do you propose to do?"

"Give him a better reason and a better chance to kill me," she said.

Loren lost all control and gasped.

"I have a month's vacation coming to me," she continued. "Aunt Lydia has invited me up to Wisconsin to spend a few weeks as her guest. Five of the other seven beneficiaries live in the Dennison area. I am going up there this summer to make a target of myself. This is one reason I need you. I know you've been involved in all sorts of, well, detective things, investigative things."

This is a dream, Loren tried to tell himself. *I've fallen into a Kafka nightmare and I can't wake up.* "Heather, please," he said. "Take a step back. Think through what you've just told me. Even granting you're right that one of the seven is a murderer and that it's one of the five who live around Dennison, why will your going there give him a better reason to want you dead?"

"Oh, of course it won't," she replied as if acknowledging that two and two made four. "Unless while I'm there I announce that I've fallen in love with a wonderful man and we'll be married before December."

That was the moment when Loren finally understood. He felt his heart pounding wildly and went rigid with the fear that he was having a coronary.

"By we," Heather added, locked in her own world, seeing nothing of his anguish, "I mean the two of us. Loren, will you do this for me and for the women and children I serve? Please?"

THREE

Loren lived the next hour in a blur as Lydia Dennison herded him around the ballroom in frenzied spirals, introducing him to one cluster of guests after another, names, nods, ritual handshakes, interspersed with merciful pauses in which he might sip Irish on the rocks from the glass with a swirling golden D monogram in his left hand or snatch a bite of finger food from a passing server's tray, munching a hot cheese puff or mushroom tartlet amid the factory machinery roar of a hundred fifty voices, then on to another round of introductions. "George Gleason, CEO at Nature's Ovens, Professor Mensing." Sunlamp tan, lantern jaw, smartly tailored gray suit, long oily hair drawn back in a ponytail. "Professor Mensing, meet Ward Dennison, a nephew of my husband." A name Loren recognized from the family tree as the oldest of the surviving beneficiaries: thick hair the color of dirty snow, Lincolnesque stoop, grave smile like a funeral director welcoming mourners to a wake. "Ward, you haven't seen Phil Clift here, have you? He was at the concert and said he'd probably be a little late but he'd try to come . . . Professor Mensing, my grandniece Angela and her husband Charles Pardee. Charlie, have you seen Phil?" The woman looked stunning in a cocktail gown made to display beautiful breasts, her smooth milk-chocolate skin telling proudly of parents from different races. The man at her side, who Loren gathered was an instructor at Dennison Community College, had white-blond hair and a weak chin and stood six inches shorter than his statuesque wife. "And this is Anders Nordsten who's here on a grant from the Danish government to study our Alpendenn plant's techniques for producing European cheeses. *Herr Nordsten, hier ist Professor Doktor Loren Mensing, ein sehr vornehmer Jurist.*" Flash of teeth bright as if he painted them every morning, handgrip like a strangler's. "Good to know you. *Ich bin Dansker, ich spreche Englisch nur ein bisschen. Können Sie Deutsch?*" And on and on through the kaleidoscope until Loren felt so dizzy he was afraid he might keel over.

Then suddenly Lydia took his hand and strode with him in tow to the dais at the ballroom's far end, her free hand beckoning as they shot past the alcove with the four brocaded chairs. Heather came hobbling forward on her thick black cane as her tireless great-aunt tapped a fiery fingernail against the mouthpiece of the portable microphone unit that had been set up on a fragile antique t.able, adjusting the volume control until the mike emitted an ear-splitting screech and the small talk of dozens of reception guests turned instantly to silence.

"My dear friends," she said into the mouthpiece, "makers of magnificent music, lovers of magnificent music, members of my family, colleagues in the work of the family, and those of you who are just here because I throw a damn good party." She paused for the burst of polite laughter she knew would come. "Tonight we celebrate the triumphant end of yet another series of subscription concerts by the Dennison Chamber Ensemble." Another pause, this time for the expected clapping response. "And once again we thank with all our hearts those who made such beauty possible: the performers of course, and Dan Feinberg and his staff at the Dennison Cultural Foundation, and everyone else who helped and supported our cause." The clapping boomed like thunder and Lydia waited till it died away. Her timing and intonation were so perfect Loren began to wonder if she'd ever been on the stage.

"But tonight," she went on, "I have a special and personal reason to rejoice." She nodded for Heather to stand at her right side and Loren at her left. "And that is to announce the engagement of my beloved grandniece, Heather Dennison of New York City, and the distinguished professor of law, Mr. Loren Mensing." As the roar of obligatory applause spread over the ballroom, Lydia stepped to one side and Loren and his future bride came together with arms around each other's waists. Stroking her left hand with his own, Loren felt the thickness of her cane and the shape of the heavy ring he'd been too distracted to notice in the Volvo or the alcove. "I'll be wearing it when you see me in Dennison," she had told him in their last long-distance phone conversation before he'd set out for Wisconsin. "It's the one my father gave my mom but nobody here has ever seen it." He played his part to the hilt, bobbing his head in acknowledgment of the applause, nuzzling Heather's cheek as he held her close. Lydia moved between and in front of them and all three embraced like a family group posing for a photographer. Then the vivacious old woman stepped forward again to the microphone. "And now, as I understand they say in New York, enough already! Enjoy the party!"

Amid more clapping the trio made their way back from the dais to the secluded alcove, which was empty now. Obese Clay Brean had either joined the throng of standees or left and Miles Lewis was just being taken away by a thick-chested, square-chinned man with a Marine haircut who was guiding the old dodderer with the implacable gentleness of a male nurse in a geriatric clinic. "Barney! Barney!" Lydia called as she hauled Loren over to the two. "Loren Mensing, this is Barney Lewis, our district attorney and Miles' son. I just had to introduce the only two lawyers in the room."

"Pleasure, Professor," Barney said. "I thought I recognized your name when Mrs. Dennison was doing the honors up there. I believe you've helped crack a crime or two between law school lectures."

Loren froze. It was the last aspect of his life he wanted mentioned in this town, and Barney Lewis had a voice like a drill sergeant's. "I'm afraid you were told some tall tales," he said, hoping in desperation that the dull roar of the party would keep others from overhearing them. "I've been lucky once or twice."

"Didn't sound like luck to me." The younger Lewis flexed his left shoulder against which the older nestled. "I have to take Pop home. Will you be around long?"

"I'm giving him the grand tour tomorrow," Lydia announced without so much as a glance in Loren's direction.

"Drop him off at my shop around twelve-thirty and I'll let the taxpayers treat us to lunch. Nice meeting you, Professor." Adjusting his grip around Miles Lewis' waist, the prosecutor shepherded his father towards the ballroom doors. Loren thought of the alternate versions of his own future, the vibrant woman brimming with life and the disoriented old man trailing drool from a corner of his mouth. "I know," Lydia whispered into his ear as if she could read his mind, and led him back to the alcove.

The moment she sank into one of the chairs, she kicked off her black silk pumps and wiggled her toes luxuriously. "Relax, kids," she said. "We're off duty." A server ventured into the alcove and Lydia beckoned him close. "Perfect timing," she told him. "Sherry for me, a big one. Heather, diet soda still?"

"Irish. Rocks," Loren added.

49

"And snacks for three," Lydia ordered. "The cook's off today," she explained to Loren, "and I never have a real meal after a wing-ding. If you lovebirds want supper you're on your own." She lowered her head until it was inches from the delicate gold watch on her wrist. "Getting near seven. The caterers should be gone half an hour after the guests are shooed out. Then you get to see the real me." She flicked at Loren a naughty glance. "If I won't scare you away?"

"I doubt you've ever scared a man away in your life," Loren said. "Seriously though, are we alone here when the caterers leave?" He moved his head a fraction of an inch in Heather's direction and lowered his voice to almost a whisper. "Suppose the man who attacked her comes back?"

"Come with me." Lydia rose and padded in stocking feet to the bay window with Loren at her heels. "See that building?" He peered out at a long white clapboard structure two stories high and apparently with three front doors. "In the old days that was the coach house. Almon had it remodeled into three apartments for the servants around 1950. Very spacious and comfy, a loft bedroom on the upper level in each unit." She paused for effect: actress training again? "A gentleman named Luther Fraser lives in the middle unit. At odd moments he has a bizarre sense of humor. He protected Carter and Reagan when he was in the Secret Service. Now he protects me. I keep a panic button on my bedside table that's connected to him 24 hours a day. A state-of-the-art alarm system protects this house. You see, we don't have much violent crime in Dennison but for better or worse I am the queen bee of the community and I know there are sociopaths out there. Satisfied?"

"Relieved anyway." Loren stepped back from the bay window. "I'm curious why your Secret Service man isn't in here covering the party." Then he realized he'd made an assumption with no facts to support it. "Or is he?"

Lydia's eyes crinkled with silent laughter. "He's wearing a tux of the same model as the real catering people. I distinctly saw you take a mushroom tartlet from his tray while I was showing you off." She touched Loren's arm with a firm gentle hand. "I know you're concerned about Heather after what happened Tuesday night but she's as safe here as I am and much safer than most Americans these days." They returned to the brocaded chairs, one sitting on each side of Heather as if to shield her from the world outside the womb of this alcove. Lydia raised the water tumbler filled with sherry that the server had left while they were at the window.

"To you," she said, gazing at Loren with a look of loving acceptance that made his eyelids sting. "Welcome to our family."

It was a few minutes before eight when the panel truck from the catering service passed under the stone archway into dusk. Loren watched its taillights vanish from the front window of a long narrow room paneled in glistening oak. The security guard had programmed the alarm system and said goodnight. Lydia had excused herself: "Three miles on the treadmill, some laps in the pool, a long hot bath and pajamas. I'll join you for a nightcap around nine-thirty. Another soda for Heather I suppose, hot milk for me . . . Are we Dennisons decadent broads or what?" Loren and Heather were alone.

"How much does she know?" he demanded.

"Nothing from me." Heather was sitting with her cane across her knees in one of twin recliner chairs that faced a six by eight foot pull-down screen at the room's far end. Halfway between the chairs and the screen stood a massive cube of polished teakwood with what looked like double doors at either end. Wondering why Lydia would have a modernistic sculpture plunked down in the middle of traditional decor, Loren crossed the room and dropped into the vacant recliner.

"Why do I have the feeling she knows we're not engaged but doesn't care we're here on false pretenses? That she supports us no matter what game we're playing?"

"Loren, you're imagining things." Heather frowned, lips pressed tight, fingertips drumming on her cane. "Aunt Lydia's a very wise woman. She doesn't flaunt it but she just naturally projects self-assurance, being in charge in an easy unthreatening way. That's all you've sensed." She pointed the cane's tip at one of the high bookcases that dotted the walls of the room. "You can see her coming across that way even fifty-five years ago when she was in movies."

That was when Loren first noticed that the bookcase Heather had indicated and every other one in the room as well were filled not with books but videocassettes. "She was in movies," he repeated, congratulating himself that his hunch about Lydia was almost right. "That gizmo's not a wood sculpture, it's hollow, isn't it? With a VCR and video projector inside. This isn't a library or study, it's a screening room."

"When Almon was alive he and his cronies would smoke cigars in here and play billiards or bridge. Lydia likes to curl up with a couple of old movies when she doesn't have a social engagement at night."

"I've watched a fair number of old movies myself," Loren said, "but I don't recall a Lydia Dennison. Oh, of course, she must have been in pictures before Almon married her. What was her maiden name?"

"Schmetzner I think she said. Her parents were German immigrants." *I should have guessed that,* Loren thought. "But her professional name in Hollywood was Betty Stewart."

"Doesn't ring a bell either," Loren confessed.

"She wasn't in the business too long, something like from 1937 till 1942. Mainly she had unbilled bits in major pictures and bigger parts in quickie Westerns. And I believe she was one of the suspects in a couple of Charlie Chans." With the tip of her cane she sighted on another bookcase further down the room. "Look over in that one, it's where she keeps the cassettes of the stuff she was in. She was still making her living in B pictures when she came through Dennison in 1942 on a war bond selling tour and Almon fell in love with her."

Loren uncoiled himself from the recliner, wandered over to the shelves where Lydia kept her recorded performances. Johnny Mack Brown, Tex Ritter, Bill Elliott were the male stars, and most of the titles on the cassette boxes fell into a standard pattern. *Colorado Raiders, Marshal of Ghost Valley, The Cyclone Horseman. . . .* At least thirty shoot-em-ups besides the occasional Charlie Chan and one or two low-budget thrillers. So this, he thought, was what Almon Dennison rescued her from. For him a trophy wife and the end to a lifetime of affluent loneliness, for her financial security and perhaps the semblance of love.

"I'll watch part of one with you if you like," Heather called down the room to him. "Some of them aren't bad. Lydia was a fabulous horsewoman when she was young. See the one that's called *Laredo Outlaw*? I have it set at a wonderful scene she has. Bring it over and put it into the VCR, I'll tell you what buttons to push."

Loren found the cassette, opened the front doors of the wood sculpture and exposed the video projector's huge lens. Then he opened the rear doors, exposing the projector's control panel and the VCR on a lower shelf. He inserted the cassette, touched the Play button, dimmed the room lights at a wall switch and sat again in the recliner. Sharp clear black-and-white images filled the large screen: panoramic Western

53

scenery, imaginative tracking shots of a lovely young woman with long dark hair in jeans and buckskin-fringed shirt and flat-crowned hat riding a tawny stallion along a rugged trail. *So that was Lydia fifty-five years ago,* Loren thought. Cut to three unpleasant-looking horsemen shooting at her from behind high rocks. Agitato music. The woman exchanged fire with them, her stallion reared on its hind legs and she raced back along the mountain trail as the three gunmen spurred their mounts out of the rocks and began chasing her. An orgy of running insert shots, the woman bent low in the saddle, hugging her horse's mane. Then beyond a bend in the trail she wheeled her horse around and rode straight at the attackers with guns blazing. One man went down, the other two fled and she gave chase, finally after another explosion of running insert shots roping them out of their saddles. Then at gunpoint—*Don't they ever have to reload in these pictures?* Loren wondered—she made her prisoners take off their boots, which she tossed off a convenient clifftop, leaving the unhappy pair to get back without horses or footgear to what passed on the wild frontier for civilization.

Reluctantly Loren went to the VCR, touched the Stop button, went to the wall switch and flooded the room with light, then sat down again. "I'd love to watch more of this," he said, "but we need to talk."

"What about?" Heather asked.

"Your fifteen relatives who died. I've had them checked out and there are some things I need to tell you."

He had also had Heather checked out but as to that he had no intention of saying a word.

All she had given him in her bedroom at the Auberge was fifteen names, each neatly marked on the Dennison genealogical chart with an X in red ink. That and some information about dates and places of death, photocopies of a few news-paper obits. "Did you personally know any of these people?" Loren had asked, and she had said no. How she could be so sure that some of the fifteen had been murdered defied his comprehension. At the end of the frustrating session he had taken the data with him. That night he slept fitfully.

In the morning while his coffee was brewing he dug an ad-dress book out of a desk drawer, turned to the D page and, still in pajamas, punched out a Manhattan number. At 7:40 Eastern time the man would likely be up but not yet out the door. In the middle of the third ring a vibrant upbeat voice he had first heard seven years ago said: "Domjan."

"Ted, it's Loren Mensing."

"Professor! God, it's good to hear you! You're not here in town, are you?"

"No," Loren said, "but I may be coming soon. I'm sorry I didn't call last month, I read in the *Times* about your getting a conviction in the Shelley case and meant to congratulate you. That was quite a coup."

"It helped," Domjan said modestly.

"No regrets about moving from the PD to the DA's staff?" Domjan had been a detective sergeant and a student in the evening division at Fordham Law when he and Loren had met seven years before on a case whose scars had cut deep.

"None. I still expect to celebrate my fiftieth birthday in the DA's chair."

"I may have something," Loren said carefully, "that will bring you a step closer to that goal."

Twenty minutes of conversation and they had a deal. Loren would FedEx a copy of the file to Domjan's home ad-dress and give him eight days to check it out. They would meet at the ex-cop's apartment, 2:00 P.M. sharp, a week from Saturday. "Sorry we can't do lunch but I have plea-bargaining conferences all that morning. I guess we wouldn't want to bat this stuff around in public anyway, would we?"

Loren caught an early flight to LaGuardia, cabbed to the midtown hotel where he'd reserved a room for the night. Burdened only by an attache case he caught a Seventh Avenue express subway at Columbus Circle and came up out of the ground at South Ferry, the end of the line. A lovely spring day, high thin clouds, the Battery clogged with taxis, buses, rollerbladers skimming at warp speed along the sidewalks. He hadn't seen the new Staten Island ferry terminal before. The old one from which an early Sunday boat had taken him to his last rendezvous with Kim before he'd lost her forever, that ancient structure had burned to the ground a few years later. For reasons he couldn't put into words he crossed to the St. George terminal and back. Then he walked through the haunted canyons of lower Manhattan to Chambers Street where, if he believed Heather Dennison, someone had tried to throw her under a subway.

A Lex local took him to Astor Place. He followed urine-scented tunnels to the connection with the L train, the local line extending from Canarsie to West 14th Street. The last time he'd boarded one of those trains was in 1987 when he shadowed a murdered judge's daughter across town to West Village. With a strange whistling sensation in his ears he retraced that journey now, coming out of the earth at the L line's western terminus, Eighth Avenue and 14th. A quick stop at a deli for a chicken salad sandwich and iced tea, then he wound through the corkscrew byways of the Village until he stumbled into Jane Street.

As he came near the apartment house at number 79 his steps slowed. It was here that the woman he was shadowing had been run over and killed by a specialist in auto fatalities, out to silence her while Loren was around the corner a few yards away. He kept on Jane till it dead-ended at West Street, traffic humming north and south, view of the World Trade Center towers downtown, Jersey City's riverfront across the gleaming waters of the Hudson. It wasn't quite two when he pressed the apartment buzzer beneath which on a brass plaque was the name T. DOMJAN. The foyer door gave a tormented buzz and Loren entered the lobby.

The building had been a walk-up seven years ago and still was. Attache case in his left hand, he took the stairs to the fifth and highest floor, found the remembered number, and was about to knock when the door flew open. "Hey, Professor!" Domjan's thick straw-colored hair was flecked with gray now but his voice was ebullient as ever. "My Lord, it's been a long time!" he exclaimed as he wrung Loren's hand in a frenzy. "Come on in!"

The front room gave Loren a shock. On his last visit seven years ago the place had looked like a derelict's lair, sagging chairs, lumpy couch, dust clumps, half-empty soda cans, slices of cold pizza ordered and long forgotten. Now it was immaculate with bright area rugs, books and cassettes neatly arranged on glass-fronted shelves stacked four high, windows scrubbed till they glowed, matching davenport and club chairs. "You have a girlfriend," Loren said.

Domjan pursed his lips in a silent whistle of awe. "How you do that beats me," he said innocently. "I'm involved with a gal on the PD who's got my old rank. Detective Sergeant. Worst neatness freak I ever met. I think she wants us to get married." They sat on the davenport perfectly aligned with a coffee table whose glass top was all but invisible beneath fifteen manila file folders. "That reminds me," Domjan said. "How's your own lady?" Loren looked blank. "You know," he went on, "the classy blonde private eye. Miss Tremaine.

You're still going with her, yes?"

"I haven't seen her in quite a while," Loren said simply. "There's someone else in her life now."

"Sorry I brought it up. I just assumed you two were—well—for keeps."

"It was my fault," Loren admitted. "I couldn't shake how I felt about Kim and after much longer than any other woman would have waited, Val—I don't know—gave up on me, I suppose."

"You want to talk about something else," Domjan guessed. "Let's get down to business. Your hunch about Heather Dennison was on the money. I'll take you past the shelter later if you want to see it. You're free for dinner, right?"

Loren nodded at the array of files. "With all the information you seem to have dug up I figured dinner would be Chinese take-out or something."

"Well, to tell you the truth," Domjan said, "my girlfriend's coming over at seven. I thought I'd just hit the high spots with you, give you the files so you can go over the details at your own speed. We can catch an early dinner somewhere midtown."

"It's your call." Loren settled back against the corner of the davenport and crossed one knee over the other. "How do you want to begin?"

"With the easy ones." Domjan bent gracefully over the coffee table and chose two folders, holding one in each hand so that Loren could see the typed names and dates on the labels. "Both of these guys bought it in Nam just like Heather told you. This one was Army infantry, a draftee. Blown up by a booby trap while on patrol, May 1968. The other was a bomber pilot, had his plane shot down in a raid on Hanoi, died in a North Vietnamese cage, September 1970." He opened both files on his lap and showed Loren the photographs, one atop the papers in each. "Those are their names on the memorial wall in Washington just in case you have any doubts. Classmate of mine from Fordham Law who's with the Justice Department now took them for me." Loren took the folders, opened his attache case and put them in.

"Here are some more easies," Domjan continued, scooping up three more files. "These gentlemen were all beneficiaries of the Dennison trust and they all died of AIDS before they were thirty. Maybe the old man was right about a gay gene in the family." He passed the folders across the davenport and Loren deposited them in his case.

"Now these," Domjan said, reaching for two more, "these fellows died in the early Eighties when doctors tended to spare family feelings by calling AIDS deaths something else. One was 39, the other was 42. They both stayed in as trust beneficiaries by getting married before they turned thirty. Both of them died in the closet." He handed those files over. "I talked over the phone with the doctors who signed the death certificates. They have absolutely no doubt the real cause of death was AIDS."

Seven down, eight to go, Loren said to himself. By this time he could see half the surface of the coffee table top.

"You can forget these three." Domjan moved to his lap a group of files that had been lying next to each other at one end of the table. "When Almon Dennison died in 1964, these two ladies were the oldest beneficiaries under the trust. This one was 87 when she passed away in 1973. Alzheimer's. The other died of inoperable brain cancer in 1978, a week after her eightieth birthday. The third one here is Heather's dad. He died on the operating table in 1982 during quadruple bypass surgery." Loren transferred the folders into his case. "Not a trace of our Alec so far, wouldn't you say?"

Loren had no idea what Domjan was talking about and his dead fish stare must have shown it. "Professor, I thought you loved old movies like me!" he said in a disappointed tone. "Alec Guinness! *Kind Hearts and Coronets*! Remember the English guy who was killing off everyone in the family who stood in the way of his getting a title? I think it came out in 1949. Great flick."

"Oh." Loren felt ice in the pit of his stomach. He and Kim Hale had seen that picture together at a revival house when they were first year law students, before she had vanished without a trace for the first time but not the last. He had never trusted himself to see it again. With hands clenched he made himself return to the here and now. "Alec Guinness didn't play the murderer," he pointed out quietly. "He played all the victims. Dennis Price was the killer."

"Damn," Domjan whispered, then added: "Doesn't matter. Your client's hypothetical mass murderer is still Alec to me."

"Your call," Loren shrugged. "Am I correct in assuming that those last files are the interesting ones?"

"You might say that." He reached to the tabletop, pushed all five remaining folders closer to his end of the davenport and selected one. "Robin Thorn," he read from the label. "Born 1950 in Grand Forks, North Dakota. Her mother was the granddaughter of one of Almon Dennison's maternal aunts. Robin was fourteen when Almon died. Three years later she was dead too."

"Dead how?" Loren asked.

"She was a wild Sixties kid. Loved motorcycles, bought a Hog with some of her trust money. Liked to take it out in the middle of the night when the interstate highways were nearly empty and cruise along at ninety miles an hour. One night in August 1967 a truck plowed into her from behind. She wasn't wearing a helmet and from the ME's report in this file I thank God I didn't have to look at her face. No witnesses, never any arrest. Might have been a drunk who didn't dare report it. Might have been Alec. Either way, every other beneficiary in the trust got income checks for that much more after she was dead. Here, read this one carefully tonight." Loren tucked the Thorn file in the upper compartment of his attache case, separate from the first ten.

"Gregory Dennison," Domjan read from the label of the next folder he took up. "This was the younger of the two sons of Almon's brother Ward Dennison so what does that make him to Heather? First cousin once removed? Anyway, he settled in Georgia and fell in love with a black gal who worked for the Southern Christian Leadership Conference. They were married in 1962, which you wouldn't call the golden age for interracial couples down there. They had a daughter later the same year. Both Gregory and the kid became trust beneficiaries when Almon died but Greg didn't get to enjoy his share very long. In fact he was the first of these fifteen to die. He was torn apart by four shotgun blasts in a clearing in the pine woods one night in the summer of '65. An old bedsheet with NIGGER LOVER in red paint was found draped across the corpse. Cops figured it was the Klan but there's nothing that rules out Alec."

"What happened to the wife and daughter?"

Domjan thumbed through the papers in the file. "Ah, here it is. They left the South for good, moved to California. When the kid was grown the mother remarried, a black guy, career military. They're retired now and living in Spain. The daughter relocated to Dennison, Wisconsin and the local county attorney told me a few days ago she's still living there. She's married too now, her husband teaches at the community college. Here." Loren arranged the Gregory Dennison file next to the one on Robin Thorn.

"Moving right along," Domjan said with a quick glance at his wrist watch, "we come to the only beneficiaries besides Heather herself who lived here in Manhattan. Luis Arrabal and his sister Juanita. He was born in 1948, she was born in '51. Their great-grandfather was a brother of Almon Dennison's mother. I think that means Luis and Almon were second cousins twice removed. God knows what it makes Luis and Heather. Anyway he and Juanita grew up in Puerto Rico and came here in the early Seventies. She spent her trust money getting an education, he spent his on tequila and cocaine. They both got married in time to stay in the trust money. Juanita took her marriage seriously, Luis took his as a joke. He is the most recent of these fifteen folks to die. It happened six months ago."

"*What* happened six months ago?" Loren growled.

"He fell under a subway at Times Square station. Around five in the afternoon, rush hour, thousands of people on the trains and stairs and platforms. No one saw a thing. There was enough booze and coke in his body so he could easily have stumbled and gone over by accident. Then again, maybe Alec pushed him."

Loren remembered Heather's account of the man who had whispered "Bitch" in her ear and tried to shove her off the subway platform at the Chambers Street station. That had been in December, perhaps two months after Luis Arrabal's death. Alec again, reprising a method that had served him well the first time? Then another thought crossed Loren's mind. Luis and Juanita Arrabal were Heather's third cousins, not close relatives by any means but apparently the only blood relatives she had in New York. He wondered if she could have known either of them. "Any idea what happened to Luis' sister?" he asked. "Does she still live here?"

"Wait a minute." Domjan flipped through the file. "She and her husband went back to San Juan twelve years ago. They live on her share of the trust income and work without pay as teachers at a Catholic orphanage." Loren took the Arrabal folder and added it to the others the prosecutor had called interesting.

"Now," Domjan went on, "we have one that actually died in Dennison, Wisconsin. Name of Mildred Brean. Her mother was one of Almon's sisters. Mildred married a guy who was killed in the Korean War. They had one kid, Clayton Brean Junior, who's grown now and still lives in Dennison."

"When did Mildred die, and how?"

"October 1970," Domjan read from the file. "Her brakes failed while she was driving along a twisty road in the boonies, maybe thirty miles from town. Car went over a guardrail and caught fire, bumping down a steep hill. There wasn't enough left of the car or the body to establish for sure what happened but the state cop in charge of the investigation tagged it suspicious. Nothing ever happened about it."

"One thing happened," Loren reminded him. "If Clayton Junior and his mother both became trust beneficiaries in 1964 when Almon Dennison died, then Mildred's death six years later made the boy's share of the trust pie that much bigger."

"Well, that's so," Domjan conceded. "And from this snapshot of Junior in the file I'd say he had a pig's appetite. Trouble is, the Wisconsin staties had the same suspicion and checked. Junior was a thousand miles away at boarding school at the time his mom died."

When Loren put that folder with the others the coffee table was clear except for the fifteenth and last file. "This is the saddest of the bunch," Domjan said. "Ward Dennison III, the second youngest beneficiary in the trust, born 1960. He and his dad, Ward Junior, and Ward Junior's younger brother Gregory all took shares of the trust income when Almon passed away in '64. Ward Junior's still living in Dennison. He's the only one of the three left alive."

"What happened to his son?"

"He disappeared when he was nine years old. Gone. Phfft. Like that." *Like Kim,* Loren thought. "He's never been found. The best guess the cops could make at the time was that he'd been kidnapped, raped, killed and the body disposed of. We know a lot more about pedophile serial killers now than we did back then. A case like that today, the FBI'd get involved, the media . . . Doesn't help this boy, does it? Maybe his bones are mixed with the concrete some fancy house is built on. Maybe a priest did it and the poor kid's under a rectory. Anyway, seven years after he disappeared, the Dennison trustees got a judicial order declaring him legally dead. Here, take the damn thing." Blindly he shoved the file in Loren's direction. "I don't want to think about it any more."

"There's—no way I can repay you for all this," Loren said. "You know you can count on Heather if you ever have an abused woman or child who needs a friend and someplace to stay."

"Oh, I'm hoping for better compensation than that," Domjan replied.

Loren tapped with his fingertips on the last file folder and waited for the other shoe to drop.

"Let's suppose Heather happens to be right. Suppose Alec is real."

Loren said nothing.

"I want his fucking ass," Domjan said.

The silence in the perfectly orderly room was deafening.

"You said this case may take me a step closer to making

64

DA by my fiftieth birthday. Well, I'm going to hold you to that. Remember, if Alec exists, the last person he did was Luis Arrabal. A piece of shit if there ever was one but I couldn't care less. I want to convict him for that one before anyone else gets their hooks into him. Then if I'm in a good mood I'll give him to the DAs in the other states where he murdered someone. Especially if one of those states has the death penalty. *But I want him first.* That's the only reason I invested my time and the taxpayers' money doing you a favor. Clear?"

Loren struggled to calm himself, organize his thoughts. "You want to use Heather and me as stalking horses," he said.

This time it was Domjan who said nothing.

"If Alec doesn't exist, she and I have wasted our time but nothing serious is lost," Loren went on. "If he does exist, maybe he'll kill Heather or me or both of us but you get a chance to try him for Arrabal, maybe. And you spent how many years in the seminary?"

"Jesus taught us to be wise as serpents," Domjan said. "Look, Professor, why do you care what happens to her? She lied in her teeth to you, she's playing some game of her own. She could be cut from the same cloth as Alec. If there is an Alec."

"I know she lied to me," Loren admitted. "I just can't figure why she'd want to."

"Well, the only contact you had with her before last week was when she was your student at NYU. Maybe it was something you said in class. Maybe . . ."

"That's absurd," Loren broke in. "I hate political correctness but diversity is a value."

"And Heather Dennison is nothing if not diverse." Domjan risked another peek at the wristwatch he wore on a platinum band. "Look, if we're going to have dinner we'd better get moving. I'll call a cab. The main office of the shelter isn't much out of our way. If you want to drop in, check out what I told you about her . . ."

"Just give me the address," Loren said coldly. "I think I'll eat alone tonight."

He left the taxi at Union Square and walked north on lower Park Avenue until he found the address Domjan had given him, a dingy office building whose lobby directory listed dozens of the sleazy-sounding small businesses with which New York abounds and, buried among them, the shelter. He knew from Domjan that Heather and her colleagues had several safe houses scattered around the five boroughs where abused women and children were kept and cared for but the ambition-driven prosecutor had not offered the addresses and Loren didn't need them. It was 4:50 when the ancient elevator lifted him to the third floor. He saw light behind the frosted glass of the shelter's office, twisted the knob gently. From a receptionist's desk a grandmotherly woman in a white shirtwaist with a thin gold chain around her neck gave him a warm but wary smile.

"Sorry, ma'am," he muttered. "Made a wrong turn." He took the fire stairs to street level and another cab back to his hotel and a solitary dinner.

That part he left out as he sat with Heather in the recliner chairs in her great-aunt's video room and told her what he'd learned in New York.

"This friend of yours in the District Attorney's office," she said. "I can't imagine how hard he must have worked to put all that information in your hands so quickly."

"I wouldn't bet we're friends any more. He's hoping for big dividends from us."

Heather shot a glance at the grandfather clock nested between two bookcases. "Lydia should be back soon. We can't talk about this in front of her."

"I don't plan to," Loren said. "But I want to explore some of the possibilities with you. I've done this in my head but if we go over it together maybe something will occur to us." She sat motionless in her recliner. "Let's begin," he continued, "with the possibility you instinctively reject. Put it in words for me."

"That—there is no—what did your friend call him?—Alec. All those things are unrelated. They just happened." She formed the sentences reluctantly, like a theologian conceding that there just might not be a God.

"There is only one other possibility," Loren said, "namely that Alec exists. Both propositions can't be true, both can't be false. One must be true."

"Loren, that's elementary logic. It doesn't take us anywhere."

"No it doesn't, so let's subdivide the theory that Alec's real. What I mean is," he said, as she chewed on her lip absently, "even if he is real it doesn't automatically follow that he murdered all five of your relatives who died suspiciously. It's also possible that he killed only one or some of them and then died of natural causes himself."

She seemed to withdraw deep into herself, thinking. "But that would mean . . ." she ventured finally.

"Go on, tell me what it would mean."

"The last of the five to die was this Luis Arrabal, six months ago . . . Oh, of course! You think he was Alec and then while he was on drugs he fell under that subway!"

"Possible but damned implausible," Loren said. "Look at how four of the five suspicious deaths are bunched together: Gregory Dennison in 1965, Robin Thorn in '67, Ward

Dennison III in '69, Mildred Brean in 1970. Luis Arrabal was seventeen years old at the beginning of that sequence and twenty-two when it ended. Also he was still living in Puerto Rico through that entire period."

Heather rocked silent in her recliner.

"Let's look at another theory," Loren suggested. "Alec was real, he killed some of these five relatives of yours. Then another one of them murdered him."

"Oh no," Heather said under her breath. "Two Alecs?"

"Almon Dennison disposed of his estate like a damn fool," Loren said. "Or like someone with a high opinion of human nature, which amounts to the same thing. Every time one beneficiary died, the survivors got more. It's not a stretch to figure that over thirty years more than one beneficiary was tempted. Suppose for example that Mildred Brean was responsible for one, two or all three of the suspicious deaths before her own. Then another beneficiary killed her. Or maybe she was killed for a completely different reason, or perhaps it really was an accident."

"Stop it! Stop it!" she cried out, then more calmly: "Loren, this could go on forever. You can work up any number of variations on the idea that Alec killed a few people and is dead now."

"You bet I can," Loren agreed. "Okay, let's pretend we've covered all of them and move on to your own pet notion."

"Alec is still out there," she said softly. "Still killing."

"Right. Now we can't prove that Alec is one of the eight surviving beneficiaries who profit when others die but it's certainly plausible. That gives us eight suspects. Three I met here tonight." He counted them off on his fingers. "Ward Dennison Jr., Angela Pardee and Clay Brean Jr. If I remember your family tree right, two more live around here that I haven't met. Laura Yates and B. Philip Clift."

"You can rule Laura out," Heather told him. "Where she lives in Dennison is the Pinecrest Nursing Home. She was diagnosed with Lou Gehrig's disease three years ago and can't even go to the bathroom by herself any more."

"And B. Philip Clift?" Vaguely Loren remembered Lydia asking for him at the reception, being surprised he hadn't come.

"I met Phil last week when Aunt Lydia showed me around. He runs Dennison Properties, the, well, I guess you'd call it an umbrella company. He keeps track of Alpendenn, Nature's Ovens, the cultural foundation . . . I guess there's nothing that rules him out as Alec."

"We can probably eliminate suspects six and seven," Loren said, "going by what you and Domjan told me. Juanita Arrabal has lived in Puerto Rico for twelve years and—what's the other one's name?—Sam Rosen moved to Israel in the early Sixties after his parents died and hasn't returned since. That brings us to the eighth suspect." He paused for a dramatic moment as he thought Lydia might have done in the same situation. "You."

"Me! Oh my God, Loren, I . . ."

"Suspect in theory only," Loren continued. "You were between one and six years old when the first four suspicious deaths happened. Killers are younger and younger these days but not that young. Of course," he pointed out with a smugness he couldn't resist, "you are the only one of the eight we know was in New York when Luis Arrabal went under that subway."

Her face went fish-belly gray, and for an instant Loren was afraid he'd gone too far. "My God," she said then, "he was nothing but a name to me until just now, and you think . . ." She couldn't finish the sentence. The only sound was the tick of the grandfather clock. She kept darting glances at its decorated face as if she were praying for Lydia to return and bring this nightmare dialogue to an end.

A muffled chirping sounded in the room. Loren flinched. Heather thrust her cane into the carpet, lunged to her feet and hobbled to a bookshelf where she picked up the handset of a phone Loren hadn't noticed. "Hello . . . Mrs. Dennison isn't available at the moment, may I have her call you back? . . . Oh, Mr. Lewis, this is Heather, her grandniece, we met at the party." Loren heard her gasp, came out of the recliner towards her. "Oh no," she said into the mouthpiece. "When did it . . . Yes, of course I'll tell her." The phone slipped from her hand and clattered onto the parquet beyond the carpet's border. Loren held her close, saw the trembling of her lips.

That was when Lydia came into the room. She wore a robe over a long flannel nightgown and carried a tray with a snifter of brandy, a tall glass of diet cola and a steaming mug of milk. The moment she took in Heather's stricken face and the way Loren was holding her she half ran across the room. "Darling, what's wrong, what is it?" She thrust the tray at Loren, snatched the brandy glass from it and forced it to the younger woman's mouth. "Come on, take just a little. That's better. Now what happened?"

"On the phone . . ." Heather spluttered, coughed on the brandy. "I thought you were still in the pool . . . Barney Lewis, he wanted to tell you . . . Phil Clift. You were expecting him at the party and he never came . . . They found him at Nature's Ovens. Someone beat his head in. Someone with an iron bar."

FOUR

In the center of the emotional storm in the video room Loren became aware of a muffled squawking like Donald Duck heard through cotton wool and suddenly understood that the phone connection had not been broken. He stooped and put the handset to his ear. "Mr. Lewis, this is Loren Mensing. We met at the party, you invited me to lunch tomorrow . . ."

"What the hell's going on?" the drill sergeant voice demanded.

"Your call caused an uproar. Did Heather hear you right? Someone was murdered tonight?"

"Yeah, Phil Clift, manager of Dennison Properties. Happened over here at the Nature's Ovens factory. It was you I was mainly looking for, Professor. Don't go anywhere. We need you now."

As if there were anywhere he could go with his car in the body shop almost a hundred miles away. "I'm afraid I have no wheels right now and I don't know the way if I had," Loren said.

"I'll be there with a car in ten minutes," Lewis told him, and hung up.

When he returned the phone to its place on the bookshelf Loren found Heather weeping uncontrollably in Lydia's arms and, even knowing what he did about her, couldn't quite understand why. Follow it up later, he told himself. "Barney

71

wants me," he announced to the women. "I have to go. Heather, are you going to be okay?"

"I am responsible for her," Lydia said. "You do what you must."

"This may be a late night for me."

"Call me in the morning. Don't worry if you get a busy signal, I'm taking the phone off the hook as soon as Barney comes for you."

"The—how do I get past the alarm system?"

Lydia eased the limp and sobbing Heather into one of the recliners and took Loren to the entrance hall where she pressed numbers on a security panel beside the front door. "Take care of her," he said, holding her close. "She needs you badly tonight."

He bounded down the front steps and into the drive as headlight beams lapped at him like an incoming wave from the sea.

Lone houses far from the night-haunted road showed tiny squares of light. Slumped in a corner of the back seat as the dark sedan skimmed the pavement, Loren wondered if this was the route Heather had taken when she made her impulsive Tuesday night visit to Nature's Ovens. "I think Lydia was going to bring me here tomorrow," he said, just to be saying something.

"Part of the grand tour," Barney Lewis grunted. "Don't worry, Professor, you'll get that tonight." He leaned forward to touch the uniformed driver's shoulder. "Circle the building, Randall."

"Right, sir." Brakes squealed as the sedan turned in at the floodlit NATURE'S OVENS sign. Loren saw what looked like a stained glass window above the long low structure's front entrance. The parking slots along the building's west side were empty. Three white-painted trailer trucks with the same insignia as the entrance sign were backed up to the loading dock at the rear. Laborers in smocks trundled shelved carts full of bread products into the trailers' maws and pushed them out through swinging double doors into the building for another load. Perhaps thirty cars were parked in the spaces behind the factory.

The sedan made a final right turn and pulled into a slot along the east side, between a police cruiser and a crime scene van. "Ambulance is gone, sir," the driver said.

"I'm not blind, Randall. Okay, Professor, let's go." Loren slid across the back seat and followed the prosecutor. The parking slot on the other side of the crime scene van held a late model Chrysler with the license plate SHRDZE. Lewis led the way to an unmarked door with a steel rectangle beside it. "Executive entrance," he said. "You need an electronic card to get in this way." He pounded three times and the door edged open, revealing a petite middle-aged man with a gray mustache and beard meticulously shaped like a topiary sculpture and a strawberry red scarf around his neck. "Professor Mensing," Lewis said, "Captain John Stacy, head of the detective division."

"Pleasure." Stacy held out a perfectly formed hand. "Well, not really I guess, considering . . . You staying, Barney?"

"I think I have to." Lewis took them along a narrow cream-painted corridor with prints of agricultural scenes framed at eye level on one wall and the other broken by several doors. The first two, locked, were marked MEN and LADIES. The third was wide open but the doorway was blocked by yellow crime scene tape. Loren caught a glimpse of a conference table, a bare-topped desk, a loveseat and two gloved and smocked evidence technicians kneeling on the gray carpet. Between them he could see the stains, dry red and snail-track white. He felt his stomach heave.

"Orientation first," Lewis said. "Then we talk." Loren felt better when they reached the broader, more brightly lit cross corridor. "That way," the district attorney waved his arm to the left, "is the front area where they sell bread and stuff at retail." He turned right with Loren at his heels and a glass-walled room sailed by: formica-topped tables, padded kitchen chairs, refrigerator, sink, microwave, coffee maker. "Employees' break room," Lewis said.

As they made a left at the next corridor the aroma of baking bread filled Loren's nostrils and drove out the memory of brain fragments and blood. From waist height to well above his head the entire wall was transparent. Watching the white-gowned hair-netted bakery workers hustling about their tasks, huddling over strange devices labeled MUFFIN MIXER, DOUGH DIVIDER, MOLDER, PROOF BOX, feeding loaves into the huge hearth oven he'd seen in the promotional video, Loren had the sense he was watching a movie, a documentary on the making of bread. Nothing in the procedure seemed to have been touched by the murder. Where the corridor ended at a blank wall he and Lewis about-faced and retraced their steps, past the break room, the short side corridor leading to the office where B. Philip Clift had been bludgeoned to death, into the high-ceilinged front section of the building where Nature's Ovens products were sold to locals and tourists. Walls lined with shelves not yet stocked for next morning's purchasers, tall wood-grain sales counter with electronic cash register, stacks of free glossy brochures touting the firm's healthful and delicious output. Captain Stacy stood in the center of the area with arms folded, waiting for them under the bright fluorescents. "Had a nice tour?" he inquired politely. "You have the picture straight inside and outside?"

"The basics anyway I suppose." Loren had the disquieting sense that Stacy was the professor, he himself a student about to face a pop quiz. "I don't know a thing about the murder except what Mr. Lewis here told Heather over the phone, and that hit her so hard she may not have passed it on correctly to me."

"Of course." Stacy caressed his neat beard thoughtfully. "That's next on our agenda, bringing you up to speed. Barney, could you rustle up some chairs from the break room?"

"Sure, Stace." The district attorney of Dennison County hustled off to do the detective captain's bidding like the newest probationary cop on the city force. Small jurisdictions sure are different, Loren thought. Lewis came back lugging three nondescript tubular chairs and set them down in a rough approximation of a circle.

"Now," Stacy announced, plucking a notebook from his inner breast pocket, "first I talk and you listen. Then we switch."

What it came down to, Loren concluded several minutes later, was either-or.

B. Philip Clift, a 53-year-old widower and lifelong resident of Dennison County, had supplemented his ample income from the trust fund and satisfied his workaholic tendencies by serving as executive director of Dennison Properties, Inc., the corporation founded by Almon Dennison to oversee his empire. With advice from top-echelon tax lawyers in Madison and Milwaukee, Clift spent the bulk of his time manipulating finances so as to minimize federal and state taxes on the trust properties. But it was also part of his job to supervise the three main units of the

Dennison domain—Alpendenn, Nature's Ovens and the Cultural Foundation. He kept his headquarters in a luxurious suite on the top floor of Dennison Hall but also maintained an office at Alpendenn and here at the bread company, and once a month like clockwork he would conduct a meeting with the hands-on managers of each of the empire's major units. "His last session out here was Monday afternoon, six days ago," Stacy said, his Vandyke brushing the pages of his notebook.

"Who attended?" Loren asked.

"George Gleason, the CEO, and the four MBAs who report to him."

An image from Lydia's party flashed into Loren's memory: burnished tan, Jay Leno jaw, expensive suit, ponytail. "Go on," he said.

According to the maintenance staff at Dennison Hall, Clift had entered the building shortly before noon that morning and taken the elevator to his office on the top floor. He had been carrying a bulky attache case with him. Apparently he had worked alone at his desk until the chamber concert began at two. Many of Dennison's music-loving set had seen him at the performance. Whether he had stayed to the end of the concert wasn't clear. At some time in mid-afternoon he apparently had left Dennison Hall and walked the half mile to the high-rise condominium that had been his home since his wife's death from breast cancer five years ago. The doorman told police he'd been carrying a bulky attache case. At around 4:30 the same doorman had seen Clift's auto, a 1994 Chrysler Town Car with vanity plate reading SHRDZE, emerge from the building's underground garage and drive off.

"Rimsky-Korsakov," Loren muttered under his breath. Then, realizing that Stacy and Lewis were staring at him as if he'd gone crazy: "The license plate. It has to be a creative spelling of 'Scheherazade.' " Both men still stared at him blankly. "It's a famous symphonic poem by Nicolai Rimsky-Korsakov, a 19th-century Russian composer," he explained very slowly like a teacher in a school for the brain dead. "Forget it. The point is his car is out in the lot now, about as close as you can park to the executive entrance. Therefore he must have entered the building through that door with his electronic card."

"We did figure it that way ourselves," Stacy said. "This retail sale operation closes at two on Sundays and the front entrance is locked tight so he couldn't have come in that way. And none of the bakery workers in back saw him come in through the loading dock entrance they use for themselves. Besides, he must have been heading for the Dennison Properties office which is just a few feet down the corridor from the executive entrance so why would he have gone in any other way?"

In any event, Stacy went on, he had unlocked the door of that office and stepped inside. That was his last act on earth. Someone else had been there first. Someone who had stood behind the door and, the moment Clift entered, had beaten the back of his head to mush with a crowbar or some other kind of steel club. Whether Clift had brought anything into the building, whether the killer had taken anything out besides himself and the weapon, remained a mystery. The only point Stacy was sure of was that he'd left by the executive entrance. "You don't need a card to get out that way, only in." None of the bread makers on duty had noticed a second car near the side door and in fact none could say with certainty what time Clift had parked his Chrysler there. The body had been found at 7:12 P.M. by the woman from the maintenance service who unlocked the Dennison Properties office every evening to see if it needed tidying up. Preliminary medical tests fixed the time of death as roughly between four and six in the afternoon.

"All right, Professor, there you are." Stacy shut his notebook and stuffed it back in his breast pocket. "If you were in my shoes, how would you size the thing up?"

Loren squirmed in the tubular chair that was too small for him and tried to organize his thoughts. "I can see two possible scenarios," he said finally. "Number one: Clift came out here for some reason that's irrelevant to us and had the bad luck to interrupt a prowler."

Barney Lewis, sitting Eisenhower-style on an armless chair, chin nested in his palms, forearms along the top of the chair's back, stamped his feet as if he were cold. "Give us a few more details on that one if you would."

"Well," Loren said, "since the store here was open until two, a prowler could have hidden in the rest room or somewhere till everyone but the baking people in the back were gone. That puts him in the building. What he's looking for is anyone's guess. Cash, secrets of healthy bread making, whatever. But it seems likely this wasn't his first unauthorized visit. Remember what happened in the parking lot Tuesday night? That attack was by a man with a steel club too."

"Very good." Stacy bobbed his perfectly formed little head in controlled approval. "Now do you see any weak spots in that scenario?"

"Yes," Loren admitted. "It doesn't explain how the killer got inside the Dennison Properties Office before Clift did. The door is kept locked and you need a key to get in, right?" The others nodded. "So you tell me, who had keys?"

Stacy consulted his notebook again. "Clift himself. The maintenance company. And Lydia Dennison."

"And what was kept in that office?"

"Nada. Zilch," Lewis replied. "It wasn't a working office, more like a glorified conference room."

"So that makes two weak spots," Loren said. "Scenario number one doesn't tell us how the killer got into the office or what he wanted in the building that was so important he made two sneak visits in the same week."

"Shall we move on to number two?" Stacy suggested.

"This one I like better. Clift didn't come out here this afternoon by chance. Lydia saw him at the concert and he told her he expected to be late for her cocktail party. This suggests to me that he had an appointment, almost certainly with someone who works or has connections here. Remember, part of his job at Dennison Properties is to be a watchdog over the family holdings. Suppose he found evidence that a Nature's Ovens executive was embezzling, selling trade secrets, whatever. Suppose he offered this person a chance to explain and make restitution before he went to the authorities. Now this person is desperate. He came out here Tuesday night, let's say to destroy or sanitize some incriminating paper trail, when he ran into Heather and clubbed her with an iron bar. Suppose he came early for his appointment with Clift today, bringing the same crowbar with him."

"You say you like this theory better than the prowler scenario," Lewis cut in. "Mind telling us why?"

"Three reasons. It takes happenstance out of the picture. It makes the murderer's entry into the building easier to account for: he came in the same way Clift did, with an electronic card. Also it explains why none of the bread-making people saw another car near Clift's in the lot. When Clift parked his Chrysler, if he'd seen the car of the person he had the appointment with already here, the murderer would have lost the element of surprise. Of course the killer had to get out here somehow. Captain, you might have your crew look for

anyone who might have noticed either a car parked in a secluded spot within walking distance from here or a person
being dropped off near the building this afternoon."

"Oh, we're way ahead of you, Professor," Stacy told him.
"It's being done."

"Also of course you'll want a list of everyone who had an
electronic card for that side door."

"Have it already," Stacy said. "Seven people had cards.
Phil Clift, George Gleason, the four MBAs, and of course
Lydia Dennison."

Loren shut his eyes, tried to recapture the moment at the
party when Lydia had introduced him to Gleason and the two
men had shaken hands. Was Loren at that moment looking
into the eyes of a person who had just committed a brutal
murder? Then he recalled what Stacy had told him about the
probable time of Clift's death: it might have happened not
before the party but after.

"Gleason and the quartet will be fielding the tough questions tomorrow," Stacy went on. "And I'll have to pay a call
at our stateliest home and ask Mrs. Dennison whether
anyone might have borrowed her card." Loren still had his
eyes closed. "Professor? You with me?"

"Oh, yes." Loren came to life again, blinking behind his
glasses. "The question that bothers me is, why?"

The instant silence in the room was deafening.

"Why am I here?" Loren demanded. "Everything I've suggested you thought of long before me, but you send for me as
if you're the baffled idiots from Scotland Yard and I'm
Sherlock Holmes."

"Oh. Oh yeah. Well, that was my doing, Professor."
Barney Lewis coughed once and then seemed unable to stop.
"Back at Lydia's party, when she introduced us and I said I'd
heard a few things about cases where you'd been a big help to

the cops, you didn't look like a happy camper. Remember that?" Loren waited for the other shoe to drop. "Where I'd heard those things was in a phone call I had a few weeks ago. From an ADA in New York City, ex-cop, name of Domjan."

Loren sat still, scanned his memory of that Saturday afternoon at 79 Jane Street. Had Domjan mentioned getting in touch with the Dennison County DA? For the life of him Loren couldn't remember, and quietly cursed himself.

"Crazy sort of call," Lewis continued. "This Domjan talked about the possibility there was a serial killer, someone he liked to call Alec, who was a beneficiary under Almon Dennison's trust and was systematically wiping out other beneficiaries to make his own share that much bigger. According to Domjan, your girlfriend was one of those beneficiaries and thought someone was stalking her so she told you and you told him and he told me. Wanted me to fax him everything we had on the two incidents that happened out here. Ward Dennison's boy dropping off the planet in '69 and Clay Brean's mother going over the cliff in her car a year later. Well, I believe in professional courtesy so I obliged this Domjan but frankly I thought he was a hotdog, you know, always sniffing around for the blockbuster case that will make him a legend, so I didn't take it seriously. What happens next? Your girlfriend comes out to spend some quality time with Lydia and has a close call Tuesday night. Five nights later, Phil Clift buys it. So maybe there's an Alec after all, huh, Professor?"

"There's more than that," Loren replied calmly, and told them of the two old ladies who had attacked him with baseball bats in the morning's thunderstorm. "I simply can't figure how that ties in," he concluded. "Whoever this Alec is, he can't be a pair of women in their seventies."

"I wouldn't rule out anything at this stage," Lewis said. "If Alec was behind what happened to you, stop and think what it means. If you die before Heather marries you, unless she has another guy in the bullpen and marries him right away she's out of the trust on her next birthday. Put it another way, Alec gains just as much by doing you as he would by doing her. So watch your ass, Professor."

Loren sat immobile as a Buddha while his thoughts roiled. Barney Lewis had referred to Heather as Loren's girlfriend twice, and had spoken in passing about their marriage, each time with a perfectly straight face and not a hint of irony. Clearly Domjan had not told his fellow prosecutor everything but why in the world would he have held back? Loren put it down to his crypto-religious urge to be wise as a serpent, to reserve something for his knowledge alone.

"Look," Lewis growled. "I've had some love in my life too. In your position I'd probably be doing exactly what you are. But don't you think we need to make a deal?"

"What sort of deal?"

The question seemed to bring on in Lewis another coughing fit. "I haven't been a cop since I graduated law school," he managed to say between spasms. "Stace, how should we handle this?"

Stacy sank his beard in his shirt front as if he were meditating. "My money's still on scenario number two," he said when he came out of his trance. "Tomorrow I cook Gleason and the MBAs over a slow fire and an accountant comes out here to examine financial records. Cop instinct tells me someone was skimming money and went panicky when Clift started closing in. But I'm human. My instinct could be off. If there's a serial killer in Dennison we have to be cagier than he is."

"What does that mean specifically?" Loren demanded.

"It means I'm relying on you to be Heather's bodyguard. Also to nose around, which you'll do anyway, and report anything you find to me."

"And the other possible targets?"

"Well, that's a dilemma. If Alec exists he's one of the surviving beneficiaries, yes? I put tails on everyone, I scare him off but he's never caught. I put tails on no one, I open the door for him to kill again. If he exists. Fun life being a cop," he sighed.

"Stace'll handle it right." Lewis wriggled out of his chair and stretched. "I'm going home. I'll drop you at Lydia's."

Loren fought not to react. "I'm—staying at the Cheese Country Inn," he muttered, feeling absurdly like a child caught doing something forbidden. "Executive wing," he added inanely.

"Oh? I hadn't thought of Mrs. Dennison as such a puritan." Stacy pierced Loren with a fierce stare that seemed powerful enough to draw out another's deepest secrets. "Or is it that our leading citizen has her own designs on the young lady . . ."

"Stace!" Lewis hissed furiously.

For a moment that might have lasted hours, none of them spoke, none of them moved.

When the prosecutor turned from Stacy and spoke again, Loren had the sense that a safety valve had been opened. "I guess this hasn't been one of your easiest days, Professor. Stace needs to hang around till the crime scene people are done but we don't. Come on, I'll have you at the hotel in fifteen minutes."

Everything was the same, the sedan, the night-bound roads, the silence, the darkness broken by distant lights, only this time Lewis did his own driving and Loren sat beside him in the front seat. What cut the silence was another spasm of coughs from the prosecutor that Loren put down to nervousness.

"You have to try putting yourself in Stacy's shoes," he said when he could speak again. "He's lived alone too long, maybe been a cop too long. Chicago's where he put in most of his time before we hired him here, well, you know, the shit overpowers you after a while. You have to spew the poison out."

Loren saw a cluster of lights ahead and thought he recognized the general area. They were nearing the only home he had tonight.

"You academics never get to see what we do," Lewis went on. "The walking garbage out there . . . Sometimes I think Stacy made a deliberate choice to take some of that inside himself, so he could save the decent people from the cannibals."

"Not to mention saving that grand old Norman Rockwell atmosphere everyone seems to be selling around here," Loren said.

"Would you rather deal with the Alecs on your own?" Lewis swung left, climbed a rise, turned right into the executive wing's lot. "Hang in there, friend," the prosecutor said, holding out his hand in the dark cell of the front seat. "My offer to buy you lunch tomorrow's still open."

"I may still be in dreamland at lunchtime." Loren tried but failed to hold back a yawn. "I'll call you. Thanks for the lift."

" 'Night."

As he rooted in his pockets for the key and trudged towards the dim-lit entrance he had just enough presence of mind left to glance at the handful of cars parked in adjacent slots at the side of the executive wing. Four in all. Three bearing license plates with conventional number-letter combinations, the fourth reading JSBACH. He was too exhausted to remember if he'd seen that one before.

FIVE

The last thing he did before collapsing into the king-size bed was to take the phone off the hook. The two valiums he had gulped down with tap water the moment he was deadbolted inside his suite put him under before he had time to tune the nightstand clock radio to KDEN. When the grogginess wore away and he realized it was daylight he fumbled for his glasses, shut his left eye, focused his right on the clock's digital numerals and found it was 7:46. Taking one thing with another, not a bad night's sleep. He couldn't remember if he'd dreamed. After replacing the handset where it belonged he was halfway to the bathroom when the phone rang and he leapt for it. "Hello?"

"Mr. Mensing, this is Lydia Dennison." Her voice had lost its soothing quality, degenerated into a sort of hoarse croak. "Forgive the way I sound, I didn't sleep much. Heather and I were awake most of the night."

"Is she all right?"

"She's sleeping like an infant now. Mr. Mensing—Loren—I need to see you at once."

"About Phil Clift? I'm sorry, I just woke up and haven't seen a paper or the local news on TV. If you have you may know more about it than I do."

"Partially about Phil," she said, "mainly about Heather."

Loren's mind raced, and he wondered if this remarkable old woman had discovered some secrets of her grandniece

86

that he himself hadn't learned yet. "I haven't showered or shaved, I need a bite to eat and my car is in the shop eighty miles away. Seeing you right away would be a little difficult."

"Well," she said with an intimate chuckle in her voice, "I don't know you well enough to bathe or shave you but you can count on me for wheels. May I come by in half an hour?"

"I'll be in the breakfast room downstairs. Blow your horn when you drive into the lot and I'll let you in."

"Try the muffins and cheese on the buffet," she suggested. "They're from Nature's Ovens and Alpendenn."

It was ten minutes after eight when he unlocked the breakfast room with his suite key. A bright airy room, cushioned wicker chairs, sunlight pouring in through chintz-curtained windows. Plastic coffee cups and juice glasses and plates in the trash bin showed him that the other guests who had spent the night in the executive wing must have started their day early. He poured orange juice from a pitcher, washed down his aspirin and Cardizem tablets and some vitamin pills. The cloth-draped tables against a wall offered muffins, bagels, a cheese board, cold cereals, yogurt, a bowl with oranges and bananas. There had been a platter of sticky buns but only one was left. Loren split and toasted an English muffin, popped it up when it was light brown, topped its halves with slices of cheese and microwaved them for thirty seconds. He was finishing his impromptu breakfast pizza and starting a second cup of coffee when the sound of an auto horn drew him to the window just in time to see a familiar burgundy station wagon with CALL ME A TAXI on its doors slip into a vacant slot. Lydia Dennison in tan blouse and slacks and a white sweater let herself out of the back seat and trudged listlessly toward the building's entrance as if she hadn't slept in a week. Loren trotted to the front door and held it open for her. Even with her eyes hidden behind sunglasses she looked decades older than she had last night. "Good morning," she greeted him in a low tone that was less froglike than when she'd phoned.

She seemed so frail that Loren took her by the arm, helped her up the carpeted staircase to his suite, then returned to the breakfast room for two cups of coffee. They sat at opposite ends of the couch, each waiting for the other to speak. She gave in first. "Tell me what happened to Phil Clift," she said.

Loren leaned back and gave her a sanitized version of what he had learned at Nature's Ovens, leaving out the bits of Clift's brain on the office carpet and the strange interplay between Barney Lewis and Captain Stacy. "Now it's your turn," he told her at the end of his recital. "What's going on with you and Heather? Why is she so broken up by the death of a virtual stranger?"

Lydia took a sip of coffee and turned her shielded eyes to him. "Well, after all they were blood relatives . . ."

"I've studied the family tree," Loren interrupted. "They were second cousins once removed, and unless you know something I don't, they hardly knew each other at best and maybe hadn't met at all. But Heather just about collapsed when she took that phone call last night from Barney Lewis."

Lydia folded her sunglasses in her lap, exposing bright blue eyes like tiny animals peering out from caves. She took in the suite's front room in a sweeping glance that missed nothing. "The last time I was in this suite was three years ago," she said. "We were recruiting Manya Wentz—remember I introduced you to her last night, the cellist?—we wanted her very badly for the Chamber Ensemble but she wouldn't relocate to Dennison unless there was a suitable job for her husband too so the Cultural Foundation invited both of them up here for a few days and I gave them the grand tour and made a few phone calls. The reason it comes back to me now is it was Phil who solved the problem. He arranged for an associate program director's slot to be created at KDEN with a very attractive salary and that was what we offered Ellis Carr. He moved up to the job he has now when the previous program director left to manage a classical station in Boston. And, you know, this particular suite is still where we put up visiting VIPs."

"I'm flattered," Loren said. "But why do I have this subtle sense that you're evading my question?"

"Because I am?" she suggested, and laughed. "I'm sorry, this is difficult for me . . . I, well, I knew next to nothing about Heather until she made her first visit here, early last year. This time is her first really long stay, she arrived two weeks ago, and it's the only time she's stayed in my house and . . . The most amazing thing has happened. I've never had a child, Mr. Mensing. Now I feel as if I have one, a beautiful loving daughter who's suddenly part of my life as if by magic."

Loren understood that this was not a woman he could cross-examine or rush, that she would tell her story in her own time and way. "I know from the family tree Heather gave me that your husband never had children," he said. "But he was, what, in his sixties when you two married?"

"That wasn't the reason we didn't have children," Lydia said.

Loren just sat there and waited, certain that more was coming.

"To survive in Hollywood when I was a young actress," she went on, "even to survive on the level of the programmer movies I was in, a woman sometimes had to . . . It wasn't the stars or the directors, it was the front office men. The men with the power. Cruel, disgusting men. One of them—how did we used to say it?—knocked me up. I had to go down to

Mexico for an abortion. That was in 1939. Afterwards, well, I couldn't get pregnant again."

"That was the life Almon took you out of?"

"Saved me from," she corrected. "He was almost sixty-five when we married, I was twenty-eight. For different reasons we were each of us pretty much beyond having any interest in sex. Mr. Mensing, I have not slept with a man since before I left Hollywood on the war bond tour that brought me here. No offense, but as far as I'm concerned I haven't missed much. Since Almon died, what passions were left in me I've—sublimated into music."

"Mrs. Dennison . . ." Loren began.

"Lydia." She moved closer on the couch so that for one insane moment he thought she was about to offer herself.

"Lydia, why are you telling me all this personal history? Is it something to do with Heather?" Then, as his mind began to function again: "Oh yes, of course."

"We spent last night in my room," she said. "Talking the darkness away. Crying. Holding each other." Loren fought to shut out of his mind Stacy's poisonous whisperings at Nature's Ovens. "We shared so much. I feel so close to her now it terrifies me." She paused. "I know German poetry isn't required reading in law school but . . . My parents were German by birth. In my teens I was ecstatic about Rainer Maria Rilke. One of his poems, it's called 'Archaic Torso of Apollo,' I thought of its ending when Heather and I were learning about each other last night. 'There is no eye that does not see you. You must change your life.' Something like that. I can't put it out of my mind now." Her eyes seemed to mist and Loren wanted to rush into the bathroom and bring her a handful of tissues but was afraid to break the mood.

"I told her she had to tell you what she told me," Lydia went on, "and she knows she does. Today, tomorrow, when she's up to it, she will. We both feel you know a fair amount of it already."

"I know you can't tell it for her," Loren said.

"She broke down last night. Not because she's afraid for herself. Guilt is eating her like acid. She feels responsible for the attack on you, for Phil's murder. She's convinced her coming here has, well, provoked this serial killer she calls Alec and she is half out of her mind with the certainty he will kill again."

"I just can't fathom that," Loren replied. "I mean, how can she possibly blame herself . . . ?"

"You and I would call it a wildly overblown sense of guilt," Lydia said, "but it's part of her, in her bones, her genes, whatever. It's what impelled her to go to you, beg you to pose as her fiancé, bring you here. Now she feels even more guilt than before."

"What do I do to help her?" Loren asked.

"Find that monster out there and stop him."

"He may not exist," Loren reminded her.

"To Heather he is as real as her own life."

"She obviously told you a great deal last night," Loren said. "Did she tell you anything more about Alec, or Clift's murder, or about any other beneficiary living or dead? Anything more than she's told me?"

"No. Not about those things."

"What then?" Lydia sat motionless. "Come on, what was it?"

"She . . . knows something about the attack on you yesterday morning," Lydia said. "Or at least she thinks she does. She can explain it better than I when you see her."

"Anything else?" he demanded.

"Only, well, a wild idea I had. I know how you can legitimately stay here for a while and try to hunt down this murderer and I am willing to pay any amount you want."

"I don't need money," Loren told her. "My salary at the law school is decent and . . . ." He hesitated, wrestling the impulse to open himself to her as she had to him, then gave in to it. "My father was senior partner in his own law firm. He pushed me into law school and I wasn't strong enough then to resist him. I was always near the top of my class but the professors who got to know me all said the same thing. I had a great head for the law but no heart for it. I passed the bar and worked as an associate in my father's firm for a while and I despised every day of it. I came to hate him and the practice of law equally. He was distant, contemptuous, a hard charger, a workaholic. There was a violent streak in him that I'm afraid I inherited. A law degree gave him a license to make money hurting others, which he enjoyed doing anyway. I felt myself becoming more like him every day. I got out. Thanks to a judge I'd clerked for I was offered a position as a law professor. When my father caught on that I was rejecting his path he shut me out of his life. We had almost nothing to do with each other after that. He had a massive coronary a few years later, right in the middle of negotiating some deal or other. Died instantly. He was only a few years older then than I am now. I took it for granted he'd cut me out of his will but it turned out he'd died without any will at all." He broke into an uncontrollable fit of laughter as if he were drunk. "My God, one of the shrewdest lawyers in the Midwest and he died intestate!"

"Look at all the doctors who smoke," Lydia said softly.

"Anyway my mother was dead, I was his only child so I wound up with all the money he'd worked himself to death accumulating."

"Then Heather isn't the only one who has to deal with guilt," Lydia remarked.

"How about you? Didn't you come into wealth by a stroke of blind chance too?"

She sprang from the couch and stood above him cold and hard as a bar of steel. "I earned my money the way I earned this body. The hard way! Before I met Almon I was made to live in a jungle of predatory men. I gave him my loyalty, he gave me security. You and Heather keep your damned guilt!" Loren didn't believe her: she was protesting too much. Then her rage melted as quickly as it had formed and her voice dropped as she sat again. "Heather gives of herself so totally. She deserves so much better than to be torn apart by this sociopath. Please help her all you can."

"Yes," Loren promised, and reached for her hand. "Yes, I will."

"That's settled then. Good," she said. "Now you'll need transportation until your own car is repaired. That's why I came over here in Jeff Wright's cab. He'll take me home when we're finished, then he'll return here and be your chauffeur as long as you need him. Until this is over he works full time for me."

Loren couldn't help himself. Once again he all but doubled over with laughter. "You . . . really did . . . call me a taxi," he managed to say between gasps of glee.

"And if you're going to nose around after this murderer you'll need a cover story. Well, I have one for you. I'm engaging you to study the properties that belong to the Dennison trust—Alpendenn, Nature's Ovens, the cultural foundation, everything—and write a report on how the trust's administration might be improved."

"That's nice," Loren said. "I like that. But I should think it's the trustees who ought to be engaging me."

"They will," she said, and stood up again. "Now I must go home and think and try to sleep. What time would you like Jeff to pick you up?"

Loren glanced at his watch. "Not till ten anyway. I need time to think too." They took the stairway to the front entrance and shook hands outside the door as the burgundy cab backed out of its slot and the gray-thatched black driver gave Loren a flippant salute.

He was helping her into the back seat when something occurred to him that had slipped through his mind's cracks until this moment. "Before you go," he said, "do you know who drives a car with the vanity plate JSBACH?"

"Not offhand. Why do you ask?"

"Because I saw that car parked outside your house yesterday afternoon," he told her, "and then right out here last night."

When the Ford wagon swerved into the executive wing's lot for the third time in less than eighteen hours, Loren was waiting in the bright sun with a slender attache case in his hand. "Morning, sir," the black driver greeted him. "Miss Lydia says I should take you anywhere you want to go till your car's fixed so I figure we should know each other's names. Mine's Jefferson Wright."

"Loren Mensing." They shook hands and Loren slid into the spacious rear seat. "Mrs. Dennison was all right when you dropped her back at her house?"

"Wore out some is all. Nothing wrong with her a long nap won't cure. Now where would you like to go first?"

"Downtown," Loren said.

The business center of Dennison was six blocks long and six blocks wide, with enough cars on the streets and people on the sidewalks to suggest a healthier economy than most small cities in the Midwest. Jeff Wright kept up a running commentary like a tour guide on a sightseeing bus as he maneuvered the cab up one street and down another and Loren followed along on the city map he'd found in a table drawer in his suite. "On your left is the County Court House. We had ourselves a real wing-ding hundredth birthday party for that old relic couple years ago." So much for finding Barney Lewis' office, Loren thought as the cab swung left. "This here's the Historical Square. See the two statues in the middle with the pigeon shit on their heads? The one with the ribbon in his pigtail is Hiram Dennison, our first mayor. The fellow with the fancy suit and the fedora and walking stick, why that's his grandson Almon, Miss Lydia's husband." Loren wondered what the cabbie would say if he knew that copies of Almon's family tree and testamentary trust were in the attache case at his passenger's feet.

Three blocks south of the courthouse Wright waved a hand at a tall white-pillared building Loren remembered from the promotional video. "There's Dennison Hall. You said yesterday you admired chamber music, maybe you ought to go in the ticket office and get you a schedule, find out what's playing while you're in town . . . That's the County Historical Society Museum." A right, a left, another left. "Police Department. . . . Dennison Memorial Library . . . Here comes the old railroad depot. Used to be the station for the Chicago, Milwaukee & St. Paul Railroad, now it's the tourist center." They were at the eastern edge of the business district now. "Few miles along this way we have the fairgrounds and the winery. You ever try Wisconsin wine, sir?"

"Not that I can recall," Loren said.

"Smart man. You want to sample our local products, stick to the bread and cheese, wash it down with bourbon."

They meandered around until Loren's watch read 11:25, when Wright slid the cab into a slot on Twelfth Street across from Dennison Hall. "I'll explore on foot for a while," Loren said. "You go home, have lunch with your wife, pick up other fares, whatever." He poked into his wallet to make sure he still had Wright's card from the day before. "I'll phone you this afternoon, say around three. I might want to visit the Alpendenn plant."

Stepping inside Dennison Hall, he had the impression he had entered a state capitol building: vast rotunda, majestic marble staircase, gleaming brasswork, center space rising six stories to a dome. Instead of huge portraits of legislators, the walls were lined with photographs and plaques commemorating the renowned chamber music groups that had performed in the hall at one time or another. A video monitor flashed information about the next series of subscription concerts. Out of curiosity Loren wandered down a red-carpeted corridor and past a door marked ADVANCE TICKET PURCHASES to the diamond-paned double doors that opened onto the main auditorium. They were locked but the panes allowed him to glimpse the elegant interior with its deep-cushioned seats that reminded him of the business class section of a wide-body jet, and beyond the seats a broad stage. In the distance, at the edge of sound, he thought he could hear a piano and stringed instruments: rehearsal?

In the rotunda he found the building directory and studied it. The third of the six floors was the home of KDEN, the fourth housed the Dennison Hall management offices and the Cultural Foundation, the fifth was devoted to various entities that helped keep chamber music flourishing in cheese country. The sixth and highest floor was reserved for Dennison Properties, Inc., which until he was beaten to death last night had been controlled by B. Philip Clift. Was that a policeman in uniform gazing down into the rotunda from the waist-high railing on that floor?

Loren was on his way out and less than six feet from the entrance when a man who had just walked in veered over to him and touched his arm. "Excuse me, didn't we meet last night? You're the professor Heather is going to marry, yes?" He was no more than five-six and his hair was of a blond shade so light it looked like bleached straw. "I'm a professor too, of sorts. Remember?"

Loren ransacked his memory for the name that went with the face. "Oh yes, of course." He took the other's soft moist hand and saw in his mind's eye not the man beside him but the magnificent woman with dark adorable breasts framed by her low-cut cocktail gown. "You're Angela Dennison's husband, er, er . . ."

"Charles Pardee." A rueful grin made a slit between his lips. "Everyone seems to remember Angela more vividly than me. Every man at least. Are you picking up a tickets for the Ax show?" At Loren's politely ignorant look Pardee gestured to a glass-enclosed poster announcing an Emanuel Ax piano recital next Sunday afternoon.

"I'm not sure I'll be in town Sunday," Loren said.

"Well, you needn't worry. Lydia buys a block of tickets to every event in Dennison Hall so if you're still here you and Heather will surely go as her guests. Some of us have to pay our own way." He smiled shyly at Loren like a cat looking at a king. "I have to grab two tickets and a quick sandwich and get back to the college for a one o'clock faculty meeting. Do, do you happen to be free for lunch?"

"I think I have a date with Barney Lewis," Loren said.

"Oh, of course, of course. Well, I'd appreciate a chat with you when you have some time. Actually if you could come by the college late this afternoon, say fivish, I could buy you a drink at our faculty club."

"A local community college with a faculty club? That's a

new one on me," Loren admitted.

"Fringe benefit of Dennison living," Pardee explained. "The club is an old mansion on the edge of the campus that the trustees bought twenty years ago and rehabbed and donated to the college. It's quite elegant really. Will you come? There's no reason to call ahead, I'll be grading exams in my office till late." And without bothering to say goodbye the strange little academic trotted gracelessly down the red-carpeted corridor to the box office.

Loren walked the three blocks north to the county courthouse and found just inside its century-old doors a security checkpoint. What would Norman Rockwell have made of this? he wondered as a uniformed guard waved a metal-detecting wand over him. "DA's office?" he asked when the process was completed.

"Elevator's over there," the wand-wielder mumbled. "Third floor, hang a right."

The vintage elevator was run by a bald toothless operator who might well have been in knee pants and clinging to his mother's hand when the courthouse was dedicated in 1891. In Barney Lewis' outer office a thin efficient-looking woman lifted a phone, spoke Loren's name, allowed the corners of her meager lips to curve micrometrically upward and buzzed him through.

On the other side of the connecting door was the drabbest workspace Loren had seen since his last visit to the driver's license bureau. The desk, conference table and file cabinets were gunmetal gray, the visitor chairs a slightly darker shade of gray with hard green padding. Even Lewis' suit was gray. The only splash of color in the room was his tomato-colored tie. "Aha." He reared up from behind a mountain of papers on his desk and stretching out his hand. "You remembered."

"I seem to recall you did suggest lunch," Loren said.

"Did I say we were going out?"

Loren, who couldn't remember, stood there and blinked.

"Today," Lewis promised, "you get to see how a *working* lawyer does lunch."

The order was faxed to the Dennison Deli across the street and arrived fifteen minutes later, two huge sandwiches on Nature's Ovens wheat loaves: shredded lettuce and carrots, black olives, red and green peppers, mayonnaise, Dijon mustard, three kinds of cheese from Alpendenn. "I don't eat meat any more but you can have them add a grilled chicken breast if you like," Lewis had said, but Loren had opted to be vegetarian for the moment. Just before the delivery boy brought in the sandwiches and two black coffees the prosecutor made room for their meal by moving heaps of paperwork on the conference table to bare segments of his desk. They ate in silence until nothing was left but bits and pieces on the wrapping paper.

"Now," Loren asked over the coffee, "what can you tell me about the case?"

"Case? Oh, you mean Phil Clift. Well, Professor, you and Stacy were both right. The accountant he sent to look over the books thinks Nature's Ovens was taken for $200,000, give or take a few thou. The comptroller's confessed to skimming the money. Hasn't copped to the murder yet."

"Wait," Loren said. "What comptroller?"

"One of Gleason's hotshot MBAs. Computer nerd type by the name of Leo McGuire. Got hired five years ago and stole them blind for the last three. I wouldn't lay odds he'll confess anything more. He exercised his Sixth Amendment right to a lawyer a while before you walked in. I think we can nail him for it anyway."

Loren's mind took the new information and ran with it. If Lewis was right, if McGuire had killed Clift in desperation, to keep from being exposed as an embezzler, it meant that the hypothetical serial killer Alec was relegated to the darkness again. If. "What exactly do you know?" he asked. "What can you prove?"

"We know from Gleason and the other MBAs that at the end of the meeting Clift chaired a week ago he asked McGuire to stay a few minutes for a private chat. Before he demanded a lawyer McGuire told Stace what was said at that powwow. Clift accused McGuire of dipping into the till big time. McGuire put on an indignation act, told Clift he was insane."

"Does he admit he was supposed to meet with Clift at the Nature's Ovens office yesterday?"

"No, but Stace is convinced that's what happened and so am I. Scenario Two all the way."

"Then I take it he has no alibi for the time of the murder?"

"He claims he was home alone," Lewis snorted, "playing video games on his computer."

"No family or friends to back him up?"

"He's not married, doesn't have a girlfriend or a boyfriend for that matter. Technology does for him what sex does for normal people."

"How about late Tuesday night when Heather was attacked?"

"Same difference. No admission, no alibi. I don't have to prove he whacked your fiancée. With proof he had motive to kill Clift and with his fingerprints in that office we have enough to hold him. In time we'll find the weapon and if we're lucky we'll tie him to it."

"How nice for you and Stacy," Loren said. "No Alec to deal with."

"Not bad for you two lovebirds either," Lewis pointed out, slurping the last of his coffee. "No one's after either of you."

"So we each got attacked this week purely by coincidence," Loren summed up. "And all the other deaths in the Dennison family just happened too. Norman Rockwell rules."

"If you want to put it like that," Lewis shrugged. "Well, I have a rough afternoon ahead. Nice seeing you again, Professor. Give my regards to Lydia."

He spent more than an hour strolling through Dennison's center amid a scatter of visitors and locals, stopping here and there to browse in a bookshop or relax on a bench in the city park. On the streets he made a game out of looking for the vanity license plates with classical music connotations, seeing how many he could spot. He noticed a WEBERN, a GVERDI, a MAHLER he remembered from Lydia's reception, a GLIERE which reminded him it had been far too long since he'd heard that composer's passionate third symphony, "Ilya Mourometz." The BARBER he glimpsed at an intersection didn't count: it might have meant the great Samuel or a purveyor of haircuts. Maybe both.

Halfway through the afternoon he stepped into the revolving entrance door of the First Dennison Bank & Trust Company. At the information kiosk he gave his name and a law school card and asked if he might speak with the head of the trust department. A clerk guided him along a maze of corridors, past workstations where white-collar munchkins hunched over computers, and into the august environs he sought.

"Welcome to my shop, Professor." Smoky-haired Ward Dennison thrust himself up from behind his double-size glass-topped desk and held forth an age-spotted hand.

"When Lydia phoned this morning and said you'd probably be coming by I told the information desk people to bring you right up if you did. Sit, sit," he commanded as if his visitor were a cocker spaniel.

"I didn't know you were involved in running the Dennison trust." Loren sank into the tan leather armchair beside the banker's desk.

"Well, I wasn't the head of this department thirty years ago when Uncle Almon passed away but I've been in charge for some time now and there's not been a single complaint from any other beneficiary. As a law professor you know there's nothing illegal or improper about the arrangement." He folded his hands with patrician dignity on the spotless desktop. "Of course as a mere beneficiary, even the prime beneficiary, Lydia has no authority to engage you to look over our operations and suggest improvements but I understand you are, well, volunteering your time and I appreciate your desire to be sure your fiancée's financial return from the trust is all it should be."

That sounded like a subtle insult, as if Loren were a fortune hunter planning to live high on Heather's income, but he decided it was easier to take a deep breath than explain the truth. "I'm delighted you don't object to my looking around," he said.

"Oh, I certainly don't and I'm sure my colleagues on the trust committee won't either." As if embarrassed suddenly, he looked away from Loren and down at the paperwork on his desk. "Of course, one of them can't any more." Then, at Loren's questioning expression: "Oh, you couldn't have known I suppose, could you? Phil Clift was also a member of the committee until yesterday."

"While you're at it would you mind telling me who else is on the committee?"

"Just one other person, our investment specialist. You may have met him yesterday too. Clayton Brean?"

"Sounds like the trust is a sort of full employment project for relatives of Almon Dennison," Loren said.

"Yes, I suppose it does." Ward Dennison turned on Loren that sad funeral director smile. "Each of us who oversees the trust has a direct financial stake in the quality of our own decision making. If we're careless, all three of us are among those who pay the price. Uncle Almon couldn't have foreseen that it would work out this way but I knew him and I believe he would have given it his blessing."

Most of what Loren learned in the conference he had known before from his study of the trust instrument but some of it was new to him. Title to all the properties in the trust was in the name of First Dennison Bank & Trust Co. as trustee. Ultimate authority over those properties reposed in the three members of the trust committee, now reduced to two thanks to the murder of B. Philip Clift, who as manager of Dennison Properties, Inc. oversaw the day-to-day operations of the trust's component parts. Those subordinate units—Nature's Ovens, Alpendenn and the Cultural Foundation—had not been micro-managed by Clift but enjoyed substantial autonomy. "One of them perhaps too much autonomy," Ward Dennison commented ruefully, and Loren knew that the banker too had been briefed about Leo McGuire's embezzlement confession. The Cultural Foundation itself controlled several smaller units under its aegis: Dennison Hall, KDEN and the Chamber Ensemble. "The Ensemble of course is something of an umbrella entity too, or rather a convenient name for the twelve or thirteen professional musicians who live and perform here on a regular basis but in different groupings. Lydia would love to be able to have the Cultural Foundation support a full symphony orchestra but she understands that would be totally impractical in a community of this size."

"Music means so much to her," Loren said.

"More than you will ever know. I'm afraid if her hearing ever went she would kill herself. Did you know I was ring bearer when Uncle Almon married her? Except for him there has simply never been any close person in her life. Of course it's no secret that in her own will she's exercised the power of appointment Almon conferred on her so that the fifty percent of the trust corpus that generates her income goes to the Cultural Foundation. Alpendenn and Nature's Ovens do very nicely without subsidies but for good music there is never enough money. So she would tell you anyway."

"You don't agree?" Loren asked.

"Each of us has to deal in our own way with the grief life hands us. Music is hers."

Remembering that Ward Dennison's only son had vanished into nothingness at age nine, Loren decided to change the subject. "The way this trust is structured," he said, "has a sort of demented elegance I've never encountered before. It reminds me vaguely of the pyramid of feudalism we all used to learn about in Western Civ 101."

"Or did until Western Civ became politically incorrect," the banker added dryly. "My uncle was an eccentric, I suppose, but by far the most brilliant person I've ever known. Even if you had the legal power to improve on his trust I would wager any amount you couldn't do it. However, I'm happy to cooperate as you conduct your little survey. Please feel free to call on me again."

It sounded like a polite dismissal, and when Loren glanced at his wristwatch he understood. God, where had the afternoon gone? He asked if he might use Ward's phone and half a minute later he heard in his ear the voice of Jessie Wright.

★ ★ ★ ★ ★

The burgundy station wagon turned into the manicured grounds at whose border stood a dignified sign reading DENNISON COMMUNITY COLLEGE. Jeff Wright wove the cab past a network of long low white brick structures and near-empty parking lots. Signs flashed by, ADMINIS-TRATION, RECREATION CENTER, LIBRARY, COM-PUTER CENTER, and the wagon braked in front of a building in the same architectural style, DEPARTMENT OF LANGUAGE AND LITERATURE. "I'll just hang out in the library till you're through," Wright said. "No need for me to drive all the way out here again to pick you up."

"I didn't know the college library was open to the public," Loren said.

"I ain't just one of the public," the driver chuckled. "One night a week I'm out here takin' me an accounting course. With a mom and pop business like Jessie and me have and the tax laws what they are, I just don't have no choice."

"So how do I reach you when I'm finished?"

Wright tapped the pager hooked to his belt. "You give Jessie a call, she beeps me, I call in, she tells me where you want me to get you."

"I shouldn't be more than an hour," Loren said, and strode between tall blue spruces along the path to the building entrance. A student receptionist buzzed Professor Pardee's office, then gave Loren directions. His destination turned out to be a windowless cubbyhole tucked away off a side corridor in the rear with its door open. Amid a chaos of hardcovers, paperbacks, academic journals, heaps of memoranda and piles of miscellaneous paperwork Pardee was sprawled on a loveseat half buried in bluebooks. Seeing Loren in the doorway, he lurched free of the clutter like a monster in a horror film pushing out of its grave and extended his hand. "Delighted you came," he said. "We simply cannot talk here."

"I couldn't agree with you more." If a prize were offered for messy professorial offices, Loren thought, this one would win in a walk.

"Listen to this." Pardee dived back into the sea of bluebooks and plucked from the depths one on whose cover he had made three tall exclamation points in red ink. "This is the work of a student who has now completed four semesters of college." He opened to a page somewhere in the middle and read. " 'Hemingway's characters camaflouge their true feelings behind stoical role models.' " He flipped to another page of the same book. " 'It is Faulkner's uniqueness that sets him apart from other authors and helped him to feel accomplished with what he was doing.' God, God, God! Come on, I need a drink." He led the way through a rear door, over a grassy slope to a Victorian mansion at the edge of the campus.

One minute inside and Loren felt he had wandered into a sedate and exclusive club: reading room with deep-cushioned chairs, buzz of civilized conversations, hunting prints on paneled walls, dining rooms with tables laid for supper groups. He followed Pardee into a low-ceilinged bar and over to a remote corner where they slid into a booth. "Carafe of Chardonnay," Pardee said to the towheaded waiter who approached them. The wine and a pair of tulip glasses were on the table in front of them a minute later. Pardee downed most of his first glassful in a single gulp.

"Lovely club," Loren said. "I teach at a large urban university and we have nothing like this."

"I had a reason for inviting you," the other told him, and swallowed the rest of his white wine in a sort of desperation. "I need to talk with you about—well, about yourself and Heather."

Loren was about to take a sip of Chardonnay but sensed something in the air and set his glass back on the table.

"Standards," Pardee said. Not, Loren thought, a word one should try to pronounce after taking in so much alcohol so quickly. "My mission in life is to inculcate standards and every year I feel more and more like Lear in ruination, my world collapsing around me. But there are shtan—criteria and we must adhere to them." He glanced longingly at the wine left in the carafe, then back at Loren. "Almon Dennison established a criterion in his will. To remain a beneficiary under his trust a person had to marry before turning thirty. As Angela married me."

Still feeling disoriented, Loren tapped a fingernail against his wine glass and said nothing.

"What I believe about marriage is neither here nor there," Pardee continued. "Almon's beliefs are what count in this context. His fear of, well, of a homosexual strain in the family is well known. It is clear to me and in my view to any reasonable person that Almon took marriage to mean—well, what is commonly understood by the word. Not merely going through a formal ceremony. A relationship between a man and a woman who—well, as Chaucer would have put it, who fuck each other."

Loren was assailed by the certainty that he was in the wrong place with the wrong person but forced himself to sit still and let this bizarre monologue go forward.

"Since Heather came here to visit and her forthcoming marriage to you was written up in the Dennison *Dispatch* I have had an academic friend of mine at your university check you out," Pardee said. "You are in your early fifties and you've never been married. I have also had an academic friend in New York do a little checking on Heather. As far as can be determined she has never been seen in a social situation with a man. Frankly, Professor Mensing, I believe that the both of you are sexual perverts, that you've made some sort of agreement to take part in a marriage ceremony so the trust money will keep flowing into her pocket. And I want to warn you that if you go through with that marriage I am prepared to file suit and make you prove to a court that your marriage is—normal. If you cannot prove that, I'll petition the court to remove Heather as a beneficiary of the trust."

Loren fought back an overwhelming urge to break the wine carafe across Pardee's flushed and chinless face. *Be cool,* he commanded himself. *Be a lawyer.* He waited until he was sure he knew what he wanted to say.

"I don't know what attorney you consulted," he began, "but either he only told you what you wanted to hear or that was all you heard. Now I'm going to teach you a little law. First, you are not a beneficiary of the trust. You have no standing to sue."

"Angela will sue if I tell her to," Pardee countered through compressed lips.

"Fine. I'll assume just for the hell of it that she will. Let's get to the merits of her case. Do you seriously think for one minute that a court would rule . . . You teach Hemingway, right? Let's pretend I'm like Jake Barnes in *The Sun Also Rises*. Let's say I was sexually mutilated in Vietnam. If Heather marries me, you think it wouldn't count as a marriage for purposes of the trust?"

"That is precisely what I contend," Pardee answered.

"Did your lawyer ever bother to tell you about the right of privacy?" Loren demanded. "Do you really think our system has gone so insane that a judge could order me to strip in his chambers or have Heather and me make love on his bench or something?"

Pardee bit down on his lower lip. Loren almost laughed

aloud when he saw the bright drops of blood.

"Some standards you inculcate," he went on, and raised his voice so as to attract any colleagues of Pardee's who happened to be in the room. "Your wife's father was murdered by the Klan for marrying a black woman, you married a black woman yourself, which would have gotten you lynched or jailed in parts of this country less than thirty years ago, and you have the gall to preach to me about normal! As Chaucer would have put it, go fuck yourself. Nice club you have here." He stalked from the bar in a cold fury, walked at a frenzied pace across the grassy slope towards the complex of college buildings, and wondered whether his impromptu bluff had drawn any real blood. The years had taught him that the American legal system might indeed have gone crazy enough to order what he had pretended to believe were absurdities.

With Pardee's threatened lawsuit filling his thoughts he made several wrong turnings before finally stumbling upon the lot that served the college library and the station wagon with SACHMO on its license plate. He made his way inside, spotted Jeff Wright leafing through a magazine in the open lounge area and beckoned him out. On the drive back along a two-lane county road between peaceful pasturelands he sat slumped in the rear seat with his chin buried in his necktie knot.

"Something wrong, sir?" Wright cleared his throat as if he were fearful of intruding. "Anything I can help with?"

"Not unless you can change human nature," Loren said.

"Sounds a wee bit out of my line." Wright braked as the cab approached a rural junction with a blinking red light. "Look there." He pointed to something on the intersecting county road that he could see from his vantage point and Loren from the rear seat couldn't. "Here comes someone tryin' to change his nature from a human being to a antelope."

109

It came within Loren's line of vision a moment later, a tall Tarzan-chested man in gym shorts and a loosely flapping white T-shirt, running at the edge of the road, drenched in sweat, arms swinging wide. As he glided past the windshield he tossed an amiable wave at the cab. Before Wright crossed the intersection the running figure was around a bend and gone.

"I've seen that man before," Loren said to himself.

SIX

Life is making leaps in the dark. You must walk to point A and point B but no one cares which is your first stop. You choose A. Nothing happens. You choose B. A drunk driver going sixty smashes you halfway across the street and leaves you worse than dead. We live as long as we are lucky.

Loren might have had Wright take him back to the Cheese Country Inn. The day had drained him. He wanted a few stiff drinks, something to eat, valium, a long sleep. But he also wanted to let Lydia and Heather know what had happened this day and he knew Heather was ready to tell him the truth now.

The cab was on another lightly traveled two-lane road, surrounded by gentle meadows lime green in the twilight, when Loren decided. "Is there a gas station or a 7-11 where I can make a call?" he asked.

"In this vehicle you don't need no 7-11." Wright raised the lid of a compartment between the driver's and the front passenger's seat and handed Loren a cell phone. "You know the number you want?"

Loren burrowed in his wallet for the slip of paper on which he'd scrawled Lydia's number yesterday, then sat there helpless with the phone in one hand and the paper in the other. "I'm sorry, I'm not used to these things. Can you . . . ?"

"Give them here." Keeping the wheel steady with his left

hand, Wright glanced at the number, then touched buttons on the phone with the fingers of his right. He held the plastic instrument to his ear for several seconds before he thrust it back at Loren and said: "Your party, sir," like a butler in an English farce. Loren put the handset to his own ear and heard Heather's voice, taut with desperation. "Hello? Hello? Please, please, who is this?"

"Heather, it's me."

"Oh, Loren, thank heaven! Where are you?"

Loren surveyed the green slopes dotted with cows munching grass in the fading light. "I have no idea," he admitted. "Are you okay?"

"I'm fine but Lydia's gone."

"What?" Loren felt a gulf of fear inside him.

"Neither of us got much sleep last night. I woke up this afternoon, maybe one-thirty, and she was gone and the Volvo was gone and Mr. Fraser the security man didn't know anything. I was terrified for hours. Then around four while I was in the shower she called here and left a message on the tape machine saying she's all right, she'll be home sometime this evening."

"You're sure it was her voice?"

"It sounded like her but—just a little strange."

"Strange how?" Loren demanded. "As if someone were forcing her to make the call?"

"No, not like that." She hesitated. "I didn't sense that she felt threatened. Just that—well, it was as if something—I don't know what the right word is—as if something momentous had happened."

"Are you alone in the house right now?"

"The housekeeper's still here," Heather said. "She's getting ready to go. She doesn't live here, she has a place in town."

"Want company?"

112

"I'd give ten years of my life for yours," she said softly.

"It won't cost you a day," he promised.

Fifteen minutes later the station wagon passed under the familiar stone archway and braked at the foot of the front steps to the Dennison mansion.

They sat in the room where forty years ago Almon Dennison had offered cigars, billiards and poker to the male elite of the town that bore his name. A few minutes' scrounging and Heather had located a bottle of burgundy she assured him was not from Wisconsin and some scone-like biscuits she insisted were the fruit of Nature's Ovens. He had told her of his day, the lunch with Barney Lewis, the face-off with Pardee at which she fought to keep from laughing. He emptied himself of all he had to say.

"Okay," he finished. "Now it's your turn."

She stared vacantly at him and licked her lips. "Loren, I— I'm so sorry. I should have told you when I first came to you, I know that now. I needed you desperately and I was afraid you'd turn me away."

Loren sat in the recliner at an angle to hers balancing the wine glass on his knee, watching the burgundy reflect the lights. "Lydia told me you think I know," he said, not looking at her.

She didn't answer. She might have been a sculpture.

"Let's make a deal," he went on. "You tell me your secret, then I'll tell you if and how I knew."

She raised her own glass to her mouth as if for courage, and Loren knew she was on the brink of making her own blind leap in the dark. She drank greedily, as Pardee had before calling both Loren and Heather perverts.

"I am a nun," she told him.

He willed himself not to react but a glow of satisfaction

and contentment spread like a stain inside him. "I did suspect that from the first," he said, keeping pride out of his tone.

"Loren, you couldn't possibly . . ."

"I could and I did," he broke in. "I don't know if you wanted me to think you were a lesbian the way that idiot Pardee still does but if you did you blew it badly. My God, you'd never even heard of *Baehr v. Lewin*! That's like a black person who's been to law school and never heard of *Brown v. Board of Education*, just inconceivable. So I asked myself what else might have made you so adamant about not complying with the trust and marrying before you were thirty, and the answer popped out: suppose you were a nun? Domjan of course confirmed my hunch before I met him in New York. And when I dropped in at the shelter office on Park Avenue South and saw a receptionist in post-Vatican II nun clothes, there was living proof in front of my eyes. You really should have told me weeks ago."

"I was afraid to," she said.

Loren sensed a blow was coming and longed to refill his glass with wine to cushion the impact but kept motionless.

"Some of the things you said in class back at NYU," she went on. "I can remember like it was yesterday when you were telling us about restrictions in wills and trusts based on religion and lifestyle and all of that. You said there were dozens of reported cases of Catholics, Anglicans, Jews, Greek Orthodox, people of every religion who used their money to try to control other people's central choices but the only ones who seemed to have the decency not to do that were people who didn't believe in religion at all. I can still hear the class laughing when you said that."

"That was the absolute truth," he insisted. "There's not a single English or American judicial decision where an atheist or a secular humanist tried to use a will or trust to . . ."

"Even if it's the truth it told me something about you," she said. "About where you were coming from. That's why— well, why I decided not to tell you where I came from." She smiled at him. "But you knew and you're here anyway. Why?"

He pressed back against the recliner, drawing away from her a little, retreating into himself. "I have problems," he told her. "Loneliness. Depression. I've lost interest in teaching, I do it by rote. Life tastes more stale to me every day. You have no idea what it meant to have you come to me from nowhere and—well, get me involved in something again. That's part of why I'm here."

"And the rest?"

"After what Domjan told me about the deaths among the Dennison beneficiaries I wasn't convinced an Alec existed but it was a real possibility and I was, I guess you'd say bothered by you coming out here and sort of inviting him to kill you. So I decided to invest a week or two. My time isn't worth much to me."

"Haven't you left out something?" she asked.

Behind his glasses his face went blank with incomprehension.

"I think you enjoyed knowing about me and not telling me," she accused him. "It must have made you feel very superior and patriarchal. And what a thrill you must have gotten out of, well, teasing me sexually, like when you rubbed those two keys together!"

"I did think you deserved to be kept wondering whether I'd cracked your secret."

"I suppose I did." She tossed her cane to the carpet, slid out of her recliner and sat at his feet. "I'm so sorry I didn't trust you, Loren. Forgive me?"

He took her hands between his own and looked gently into

her pale shining eyes. "I thought you folks had a rule that you had to confess before you could be forgiven."

"But I have," she protested. "I've told you . . ."

"Didn't you tell Lydia that you thought you knew what was behind those old bitches with baseball bats who disabled my car yesterday? You haven't told me yet."

"Oh," she said in a tiny voice. "That."

Loren kept her hands between his and his lips shut.

"Let's go into the living room," she said after what to Loren's mind seemed hours of silence. "I want to be sitting next to you when I'm telling you this."

He struggled out of his recliner, went down on one knee to retrieve her cane, put an arm around her waist and helped her to her feet.

"I can make it on my own," she told him. "You bring the wine, I'm going to need that too."

They chose a davenport that faced the front windows so they could see Lydia's headlights if and when she came home. The burgundy bottle and their glasses and the forgotten scones were arranged on a low inlaid table which also held Heather's cane. "This is, it's just so hard to put into words for you," she began. "It was easier explaining to Lydia last night and she doesn't have religious bones in her body any more than you do . . . Can you imagine how it must feel if you're gay or lesbian but can't admit it to yourself, stop pretending, live what you are?"

The question forced Loren's mind back to the time he had spent in his father's law firm, despising himself, despising the work, daring to say nothing. "Yes, I can imagine that," he said, and braced himself for a shock, that she really was homosexual, that she was going to have a sex-change operation, whatever.

"This is how I've come to feel about—the religious life. The church. God. Loren, I no longer believe what I'm required to believe and it's an agony worse than cancer. It's like I'm the same as so many of the horribly abused women I try to serve, who are trapped in marriages or relationships they just cannot bring themselves to break away from."

"But your situation's unique," Loren added. "The clock keeps ticking. Each day brings you closer to your thirtieth birthday. If you haven't broken away and gotten married by then, your trust income disappears."

"Not mine. Every penny of that money goes to the shelter. If I don't stay in the trust it's those women and children who get hurt, not me."

"No wonder you were so desperate to have me find a loophole in the trust for you to crawl through," Loren said. "No wonder you don't care much whether Alec kills you or not. You're in a hole where you're damned if you do and damned if you don't."

"Don't use that word!" She snapped the command at him with such concentrated fury he knew he had opened a raw wound. They sat for a time in miserable silence which Heather was the first to break.

"Do you know what detheifying means?" she asked.

"Never heard the word in my life," Loren said.

"It's, well, it has roots in Rudolf Bultmann's call to demythologize religion back in the Forties and I suppose in the Death of God theology of the Sixties but it's different. We're small groups of men and women who are asking ourselves if, well, if living a life of caring for one another can be decoupled from the dark side of religion without being totally divorced from all religious sensibility." A tiny burst of giggling escaped her. "That must sound like gibberish to you."

"A little," he admitted.

"Here's another question for you. Have you ever heard of Faith Family & Freedom?"

"The Christian Right group? Of course, who hasn't? Didn't *60 Minutes* do a segment on them last year?"

"What do you remember about them?"

"Nothing that's any good. They're nationally organized. Aren't they sort of ecumenical in a perverted way? Conservative Catholics and Protestants standing together against Satan? I know they harass and terrorize people who work in abortion clinics. They field stealth candidates in local school board elections and where they get a majority they start fiddling with the curriculum so their version of the Bible is in and any author or thinker who doesn't kowtow to the Bible is out. They like to get books and movies that offend them banned from libraries and video stores."

"They also like to harass and terrorize detheifiers," Heather said. "We haven't gone public really but some of us meet now and then to exchange ideas and I guess someone in the group I'm with spoke out of turn or else there's a mole among us but . . . I've had anonymous phone threats in New York. Two other women in the group have had their cars pretty much demolished with baseball bats while they were parked in the street overnight. That's supposed to be a specialty the FFF reserves for the people they hate most, like doctors who perform abortions. Packages without return addresses have been sent to my apartment with human excrement in them. That's another specialty of the FFF. I don't know why they find us so threatening but . . ."

That was the moment when realization struck Loren like a hammer blow between the eyes. He sprang from the davenport, knocking Heather's cane to the floor, and began to pace back and forth in a frenzy of thought. "*That's* why you thought you knew . . . Those old maniacs with baseball bats,

118

it wasn't 'damnation and fire' they were chanting, it was 'damnation to detheifiers,' wasn't it? Which means they've connected you with me . . . So they must have been shadowing you when you first came to me, and when I drove up here they followed me."

She was sobbing quietly now, her head buried in her hands, her slender body rocking. "Oh, God, Loren, I'm so sorry I brought this on you . . . I try to live for others and others are attacked and murdered. I hate myself."

"Shut up," he said absently, still pacing like a caged lion, tossed about by an unseen storm. "Maybe you have two enemies, the FFF and Alec assuming he exists. Either one might have tried to shove you off that subway platform in New York. Either one might have attacked you last week. But if it's the FFF, what can they hope to gain? You don't play any important role in this movement of yours and I never even heard of it till tonight. There has to be a connection between someone with a stake in the Dennison trust and someone in the FFF, or else someone with a stake in the trust actually belongs to the FFF. Otherwise nothing makes sense."

"By someone with a stake do you mean one of the other beneficiaries?"

"Or someone married to a beneficiary, like Pardee. Or what if . . . ?" He swung around and stood looming over her like a tree about to topple. "What if someone has decided that God wants the trust money to go to the FFF and is systematically killing off other beneficiaries until the divine choice has all or most of it? Isn't that basically the plot of *Kind Hearts and Coronets*? And as luck would have it our code name for the killer is Alec!"

"Loren, that's, it's insane. It's obscene."

"And perfectly consistent," Loren said, "with what you call the dark side of religion. Do you know when the FFF was formed? Maybe it hasn't existed long enough to account for the early deaths in your family but it would explain the recent ones like Luis Arrabal and Phil Clift."

"Are you telling me Phil Clift wasn't killed by that embezzler McGuire?"

"We know McGuire's an embezzler," Loren replied. "We don't know he's a murderer and he claims he's innocent. What if that's the truth?" He began pacing again, lost in his own world as he crossed and recrossed the living room in savage strides. "What would someone have to know and do to be able to frame McGuire for that killing?"

"Loren, listen." Heather had stumbled over to him without picking up her cane and was shaking him out of his fit of abstraction, making him focus on the sound of a car coming up the drive. He ran to the front windows and flung back the drapes: sun sinking behind green hills in a flaming ball, the driver's door of the blue Volvo opening and slamming shut, Lydia Dennison in a tan jacket and skirt wearily mounting the broad steps. With Heather in his wake and clutching at chairs for support he made his way to the paneled entrance hall and opened the front door while Lydia was still fumbling in a purse for her key.

When she heard they hadn't eaten she led the way to what she called the breakfast nook, which was twice as large as the dining rooms in most houses, and sat them down with the last of the burgundy while she excused herself and went into the next room. Through the leaded glass of rear windows Loren saw a swimming pool one level below the first floor, a concrete apron connecting the near end of the pool with what he assumed was a basement door directly beneath the breakfast nook. The failing light gleamed on bright spring flowers in clay pots near the tall privacy fence that enclosed the pool yard.

The open swing door gave him glimpses of a vast white kitchen from which came the sounds of a meal being improvised. What emerged with Lydia turned out to be a cornbread casserole and a huge bowl of salad greens with honey mustard dressing. "My leftovers," she boasted, "are better than most people's first-times. Enjoy." She ate nothing herself, claiming she'd had her evening meal already, and listened avidly to Loren's account of his day. When curiosity led him to try some gentle probing as to her own adventures since the morning, she managed to be hugely uninformative without in effect pleading the fifth amendment, so that he couldn't help wondering whether she'd been spending the afternoon with a lover. After a while he gave up and ate his supper.

"I almost forgot to ask you," she said as he was helping her take plates and silverware into the kitchen. "Did Heather let you in on the big secret?"

"I had guessed it already," he said, "but yes she did."

"It doesn't surprise me that she didn't fool you." She set down Heather's plate and glass on a spotless butcher block counter and Loren deposited his in the same place. "And it makes no difference to you?"

"I wish she'd told me on her own," Loren said, "but no, it makes no difference. I'm still going to do all I can for her."

"I knew you would." She took his hand between her own and caressed it. "What a shame you kids can't really get married."

Suddenly Loren felt as if the temperature in the kitchen had risen fifty degrees. Lydia seemed to sense his discomfort and let his hand go.

"Oh yes," she said, rinsing the dinnerware, arranging plates and knives and forks and glasses precisely in the plastic compartments of the dishwasher, "about the license plate. JSBACH. Remember you asked me this morning?"

"Right." For a befuddled moment Loren had no idea what she was talking about. "JSBACH. He's staying at the Cheese Country Inn I think."

She laughed so hard she almost dropped a glass. "Now wouldn't *that* be the chamber music event of the century for Dennison? . . . That license belongs to my grandnephew Clay Brean. You met him here last night."

"Brean," Loren muttered, picking his way among memories of endless momentary introductions at the cocktail party. "The heavy-set fellow with the toupee who was sitting in the alcove with you? On the committee that manages the trust?"

"Yes, that's Clay. I can't imagine why he'd be staying at the Inn unless he and Dorothy are having some trouble I don't know about but he is definitely registered there. Room 24, right next to yours."

"I should have figured that's who it was," Loren muttered.

"Loren, how can you possibly blame yourself . . ."

"Because when I came down to that breakfast buffet this morning all but one of the sticky buns were gone. Remember how he was wolfing down crab Rangoon last night? I should have made the connection . . . Damn, I'm getting old."

"And very hard on yourself," she said.

"Do you mind telling me how you found out all this?"

"I am a crazy old bat," she said, "but very few doors in this town are closed to me." *Some answer,* Loren thought. "Now it's getting late and I haven't done my treadmill or laps yet and Heather can't drive you back because that monster who tried to cripple her last week may still be out there. You can call Jeff Wright and have him take you back to the Inn or you can borrow the Volvo and drive yourself."

"I don't want your car sitting out all night in an unguarded parking lot where someone might rig it to blow up when I started it in the morning," Loren said. "In fact I don't want it

122

in your front yard. Go lock it up now. Until this mess is over have Fraser check it out before anyone uses it." He looked at his watch. "It's a shame to put Jeff to work again so late but . . . wait a minute, there's another option. What's Fraser's number?" She told him and he turned to the wall phone and pressed numbers connecting him with the middle apartment in the building that used to be the coach house. The dishwasher was gurgling and humming when he hung up.

"He'll be ready in five minutes," Loren reported. "I told him to make sure the Volvo's locked up tight when he comes back. Maybe tomorrow after I have my own car again I'd better check out of the Inn and stay here."

"Do you really think Heather's in so much danger one bodyguard isn't enough?" Lydia asked.

"I have no idea. Maybe it's just that as a lawyer I've been trained to avoid risks." He gave her a gratified smile. "Maybe I'm just looking for a way to get more meals out of you like that wonderful supper. And to spend more time with you. You know, if I weren't publicly proclaimed as Heather's future husband I just might . . ." Loren broke off in mid-sentence, knowing he'd drunk too much and wishing he hadn't started.

"Go home, you lech." Lydia slapped him playfully across the knuckles. "If you're really so full of beans tonight you can always knock on Clay's door and cross-examine him."

"I just might do that too," Loren said.

SEVEN

He didn't. As Fraser drove him back to the Inn he felt the undertow of fatigue pulling him down and knew he'd be lucky if he had the energy to take his clothes off before falling asleep. The bodyguard was tall, thin, with cold gray cop eyes and a Marine brush cut. Either he was talkative by nature or he thought Loren needed to be kept awake. He told a few anecdotes Loren was too far gone to follow, something about his years in the Secret Service protecting two presidents. He explained the inner workings of the alarm system that protected Lydia's house, how all the windows were wired, how if a five-digit code number, changed every two weeks, was not pressed into the number panel next to each door of the main house or garage within thirty seconds after that door was opened, an alarm would go off loud enough to be heard in downtown Dennison. Loren knew the information was important but could barely decipher what the man was saying.

"I've got a brother," Fraser said. "Raises goats in rural Ohio. He and his wife are splitting. I think they oughta stay together on account of the kids." Loren heard nothing. He remembered to say thanks for the ride and to make sure the key to the executive wing and Room 22 was in his pocket before he stepped out of the Volvo. Beyond those simple things he was useless. That night he needed no sedative to put him out.

Sunlight slowly brought him awake but he lay still in the king-size bed, enjoying the absence of valium grogginess, concocting mind games he might play with Clayton Brean, like sneaking into the breakfast room downstairs and slipping a cryptic note between the sticky buns for the fat banker to find and be panicked by when he raided the buffet. FFFUCK YOU maybe? But when he focused his right eye on the numerals of his bedside clock radio he realized he'd missed his chance. It was already almost seven-thirty and the buffet opened at six. "Stupid idea anyway," he mumbled, and groped for the bathroom door.

Showered, shaved and dressed, he sat in the living room of the suite with a network morning program on the TV and a pad of Cheese Country Inn notepaper on his lap. By the time five minutes of local news came on he had roughed out a schedule for the day. He was about to turn the set off and go downstairs for breakfast when the perky blonde newsreader's words caught him in mid-stride.

"The weapon that clubbed to death prominent Dennison executive B. Philip Clift was found yesterday evening." Video footage of uniforms combing a wooded area under portable floodlights, of police cars parked in a clearing. "Chief of Homicide Captain John Stacy tells News Seven that the iron club was discovered in the bushes within ten feet of one of the nature trails that run through Dennison Park, approximately twelve miles beyond the city limits. Preliminary medical findings link blood and other matter on the club with the body of Mr. Clift." Silent footage of Stacy holding an impromptu press conference. "Whether the weapon can be traced to Leo McGuire, comptroller at Nature's Ovens, who is being held in connection with the crime, is not yet known. Now this message." Loren thumbed the power button as a spiel for a local furniture store began. As he expected, all the sticky buns were gone from the downstairs buffet.

His first phone call after breakfast was to Moxley's Auto Repair in Vale. "Yeah, Mensing, right, we're working on your Camry now, should be ready round four, we close at six." An eighty-mile drive on two-lane state roads to retrieve his car meant he'd have to finish whatever he intended to do in Dennison by two. His next call was to Heather.

"Loren, I'd love to keep you company but my knee feels so much better this morning and Lydia says if I let her take care of it today I may be able to walk on my own sooner than anyone thought."

"If you try walking around," Loren warned her, "do not walk outdoors alone."

"No, of course not, Mr. Fraser will go with me. You're still going to move in here tonight?"

"Yes. It will give you extra protection, frustrate that fat oaf Clay Brean, lots of reasons. I'm checking out of here this morning and I'll have Jeff Wright bring my suitcase to the house after he drops me downtown. I'll see you when I get back from Vale, probably around six-thirty."

"I'll have Lydia hold supper for you," Heather promised.

By the time he said goodbye to her it was a few minutes after nine and Dennison was open for business. He made a few calls to arrange appointments for himself, then phoned for transportation. At 9:45, with a reminder to Wright to deliver the suitcase stowed in the cab's rear, he stepped out of the station wagon in front of the county courthouse. Inside the ancient building he opened his attaché case for inspection, passed through the metal detector and rode the wheezy elevator to the third-floor office of Barney Lewis.

"Morning," he said briskly to the prosecutor. "I'll just be a minute. I want to find out more about that iron club the po-

126

lice found in the park and I'd rather ask you than Stacy."

"All I know is what Stace woke me up last night to tell me." Lewis glared out from the rampart of paperwork on his desk. "Someone phoned in a tip. Claimed he and a friend were hiking that nature trail just before dark yesterday and saw one end of a crowbar sticking up out of the brush. Called the cops because the stains on the club made it look like someone was brained with it."

"Did this caller give a name?"

"It was an anonymous tip from a pay phone out near the park. Young male voice. Stacy played the tape of the call and said he thought it sounded like a . . ."

"Like a what?" Loren demanded.

"You probably wouldn't approve of the word he used. He said he thought it sounded like a faggot."

"Gays and lesbians seem to be an obsession with him," Loren said. "Did you hear the tape yourself?"

"I'll hear it when I drop in on him later. He may be right and he may be wrong but you know, there's not much of an openly gay community here in Dennison. If this caller was doing the nature trail with an intimate buddy of the same gender, it would explain why he wanted to be anonymous."

"As far as you know the crowbar hasn't been tied to McGuire yet?"

"Give Stace some time," Lewis said.

"Another thing," Loren said. "Heather was wearing sweats when the man in the ski mask attacked her in the Nature's Ovens lot. Did the police take her outfit as evidence?"

"Our cops know their jobs," Lewis said. "Those sweats are in the evidence locker at headquarters."

"When you see Stacy," Loren asked, "will you have him get tests run? Heather was hit on the kneecap. There may be

127

stains on the knees of her sweats that you can prove were left by that crowbar."

"You think McGuire may have been the one who whacked her?"

"I've never seen the man or a picture of him. What does he look like?"

"Medium height, medium build, medium brown hair, medium everything. Put him in a room with two other people and you wouldn't know he was there."

"In other words he may match Heather's description of the man who attacked her, and then again he may not. I wonder," he said slowly, "if she could pick him out in a lineup of men in black outfits and ski masks. Her description was so vague I guess it wouldn't mean anything either way."

"Probably not," Lewis agreed. "And Bruce Unger would raise hell if we put his client in a lineup."

"That's McGuire's lawyer?"

"Yeah. A town this size without any serious crime problems can't support much of a criminal defense bar. Unger's the best we have. I hate the little bastard."

"Thanks for the name," Loren said. "I may need to see him in a day or two."

"You're not going to help that cockroach defend the son of a bitch who maybe tried to cripple the gal you're going to marry?" The district attorney's face went ruby with rage.

"Only if I find evidence he's innocent," Loren said. "Then I'll go to Unger and to you too."

Lewis gulped air in deep breaths, trying to calm himself. "Okay," he said then. "That's fair enough. After the talk I had with Domjan about you I'll trust you for a while yet."

Trotting the three blocks south to Dennison Hall, Loren squirmed within himself: his appointment with Dan Feinberg was for ten-thirty and he was already fifteen minutes late. But when he reached the fourth floor offices of the Cultural Foundation he discovered he needn't have hurried at all.

"Dan had a flat tire and came in late and now he's on a conference call," the secretary in the genteel outer office informed him. "The trustees are talking with him about what's going to happen upstairs with Mr. Clift gone and some other things that have come up." She had turquoise-framed glasses, orange-red hair and a face full of freckles. Loren wasn't surprised that the desk plaque gave her name as Mary Dougherty. "Can I get you coffee?"

He declined with thanks, sat in an armchair next to a window that overlooked a rear parking lot and tried to interest himself in one of the arts magazines stacked on a low maple table. The secretary managed to keep up a stream of conversation while tapping away at her computer keyboard. "Are you going to be in town long? . . . Isn't it awful what happened to Mr. Clift? . . . Oh oh, looks as if Dan's not the only one getting in late today." She gestured towards the window next to her workstation which also looked out on the parking lot. For no particular reason Loren glanced out the window beside his chair and saw a vaguely familiar man and woman step out of a tan sedan with a sunroof, the woman hefting a musical instrument case of a size and shape that suggested it must hold something like a cello. *Oh, of course,* Loren told himself. He had been introduced to both of them at Lydia's party. The woman was Manya Wentz of the Chamber Ensemble and the man was her husband, Ellis Carr, program director of KDEN. "That's her Cadillac," Mary Dougherty announced. "He drives a Lincoln. I guess she has a rehearsal or something this morning and then she'll go off somewhere, she does that a lot, but she'll pick him up again tonight. Do you like classical music? Actually I don't but you know what

129

they say in the old rye bread commercials, you don't have to be Jewish, oh shit, I mean shoot, please don't tell Dan I said that, will you?"

Just when Loren was about to give up and save this interview for another day he heard a click from the connecting door and Feinberg stood in the opening, wearing a starched white shirt and a navy tie with a piano keyboard motif, dark eyes burning behind bifocals, cold pipe dead in his hand, thin gray hair in wild disorder like a parody of an artist in the throes of creation. "Come in," he invited with a wave of his pipe stem. "Sorry to have kept you waiting."

Loren settled into the red plush visitor chair, opened his attaché case on his lap, set his copy of Almon Dennison's will on its surface as if it were a lectern, explained his commission from Lydia and the bank to report on possible ways of improving the trust's administration, and then started asking questions. For more than half an hour he took notes as Feinberg spoke about the functions of the Foundation, its relationship with KDEN and other cultural entities and with Dennison Properties, Inc. Loren understood much more of the structure's *raison d'être* at the end of the impromptu presentation. Feinberg was not a lawyer but thought like one, and he was wedded to the way things were.

"There's really no need to change anything," he insisted, but in a mournful tone as if he knew changes were coming that he would hate. "I mean sure, you can write your report, you can lobby the trust committee to do what you recommend, but the administrative structure that Almon Dennison put in the trust, why nobody has the power to change any of that."

"Not quite correct," Loren said. "There are a number of cases where courts have ordered trustees to disregard administrative provisions in a trust if the court is convinced that time and circumstances have turned those provisions into—well, like a cancer eating away at the trust's main purpose. But that kind of proceeding is way down the road if it happens at all. Right now I'm just exploring."

"Oh, there will be changes made." Feinberg spoke with the assurance of a prophet peering into a dismal future.

"I don't know that," Loren said, "so you can't possibly know it either."

"Maybe I know something you don't," Feinberg said. "Or maybe you know something you don't want me to know you know."

Loren tried to keep lawyerly neutrality in his expression while he wondered what the hell this demon-ridden bureaucrat was hinting at.

"Either way," Feinberg went on, "I don't like it. I have worked for nine years to have the Cultural Foundation make a difference to this town. Now all of a sudden everyone wants to upset the apple cart. All right. My father was smarter than most of his family, he got out of Germany two months after Hitler came to power. If he hadn't, I would have died as an infant in Bergen-Belsen. That's luck enough for one lifetime. I can't complain that I wasn't born a relative of Almon Dennison. I have no financial interest in his trust. I don't call any of the shots. I'm a paid employee. I can take my skills elsewhere if I have to. But just remember one thing. If you cut too deep, you'll drain away the lifeblood of this city and this whole area. Now if you don't mind, I have work to do." He didn't stand or offer to shake hands, just sat there behind his glass-topped desk glaring as if Loren had committed a crime against humanity.

He does know something I don't, Loren decided on the way down to the rotunda in the elevator. *Either that or he's the most neurotic person I've met in my life.*

It was close to noon when he reached the street and there was no one else in town he needed to see. He used a pay phone to call Jessie Wright, who beeped her husband, who called back five minutes later. "Am I misremembering," Loren asked, "or did that Chamber of Commerce video say you can get lunch at Alpendenn?"

"They have a little cafe out there. I've never tried it myself but I've heard folks say they make good sandwiches."

"Come get me," Loren said, and gave his location. "My treat."

The road curved down a green hill's slope in a gentle backward S. As the cab rounded the final curve Loren in the rear seat had a bird's-eye view of the Alpendenn Outlet Store and Dining Room and behind it the long low cheese factory. Wright made a left into the cross street at the foot of the hill, then another left into a lot holding forty or more parked cars. From the HANDEL and FELIXM license plates Loren knew at least two of the customers were local.

"You going to look around some?" Wright asked as they came out of the station wagon.

Loren was studying the building's facade, which vaguely resembled a Swiss chalet. "Just for a little while."

"Well, why don't I head over to the dining room and save us a table? They say it gets crowded here sometimes."

"Fine. I won't be long."

They separated inside the entranceway. Loren wandered past refrigerator cabinets stocked with slabs of cheese in every shade from snow white to mustard brown, past shelves that offered crackers, zwieback, melba toast, loaves of French bread, picnic supplies, postcards and cutesy souvenirs like china cows. He bypassed the line of customers at the cash register, followed a trail of painted arrows to a heavy wooden door with the sign TOUR STARTS HERE and pulled the door open. Suddenly the temperature was ten degrees cooler and on either side of him were panoramic windows all but opaque from condensation. Ahead of him a white-smocked young man with a shaven head that made him look like Mr. Clean was shepherding eight visitors along the concrete-floored passage, pausing every few yards to explain to the tourists what they were seeing. "Milk from the farms for miles around gets delivered here every day. You walk around the back, you'll see trucks with stainless steel tanks, that's what the milk comes in. We test it for quality and purity and then we pump it into one of the silos you'll see out back too . . . We start pasteurizing the milk at midnight. Heat it quick to 160 degrees, cool it down, pump it into stainless steel or copper vats. Then we add starter cultures we import from Switzerland or Germany or Sweden. Anybody know what starter cultures are? No? They're bacteria that help curdle the milk and give the cheese its texture and flavor . . . The next thing we put in the vat is rennet. That's an enzyme that clots milk, makes it get thick like yogurt. It used to come from the lining of a calf's stomach." Loren heard an *Oh yucch!* mutter from a teen-age girl in the group. "Nowadays they make it in the laboratory . . . See those automated paddles churning the milk in the vat? We use them to make sure the rennet's spread evenly. Takes maybe half an hour for it to get thick like we want it . . . Now through this window what you see is the cutting. The lady in the rubber apron and high boots is pulling what we call a harp through the vat so that yogurty goo splits into small particles. Any of you kids remember Little Miss Muffet eating her curds and whey? Those small particles are curds. Buy a sack in the store outside, try 'em, they sort of squeak in your mouth when you chew." The smallest child in the group giggled. "Cutting separates the curd from the other stuff in

133

Miss Muffet's lunch, the whey. That's the liquid by-product of cheese-making. The solid curd that's left when the whey's removed is what becomes cheese. The cutting technique varies for each kind of cheese. Soft cheese larger curd, firm cheese smaller curd . . . Now after the cutting there's sort of a rest period. Then we stir and heat the curds and whey in these large vats you see here. This is when the curds get smaller and firmer as they gradually lose their moisture or whey. We drain off the whey and the curds are ready for pressing. Some of your firmer cheeses like Gruyere have to go through a pre-press first. The milder ones like Muenster get pumped through those big hoses direct into the loaf-shaped forms you see there which are perforated with small holes to let the whey drain off as the curds press themselves with their own weight. Half an hour after we fill those forms to the top, the pressed curds have settled and take up only about half the form. See that man flipping the form? We do that to spread the moisture evenly through the piece of cheese . . . When pressing's done the cheese stays in the forms on those work tables till it's at the right acidity level. Then, look over here, we remove the forms and put the cheese wheels into the brine system. What's brine, anybody?" Silence. "Brine is very cold water with a real high salt content so if I threw one of you kids in there you'd float." More giggles. "We keep the cheese in the brine tank from 16 to 48 hours depending on what kind we're making. Then we cure it . . . No, the cheeses aren't sick, we just call it that . . . We take them out of the brine tanks and downstairs to one of the curing rooms where we control the temperature and humidity so it's just right for each kind of cheese we make. Muenster gets packaged and sold right after it's cured, Havarti gets aged a month or so, Gruyere curing takes much longer . . . Thank you, hope you enjoyed the tour."

Loren tugged open the door at the end of the viewing corridor, re-entered the outlet store and, feeling guilt twinges for making Wright wait, trotted to the dining area where he scanned the lunch crowd filling most of the tables. Not a single black person in the place. Could Wright have driven away and left him stranded here? Ridiculous. He was maneuvering up the aisle between the booths against the wall and the tables in the center when a tall rangy man sprang from his booth seat and thrust out a friendly hand.

"Guten Tag, Herr Professor Mensing! Erinnern Sie mich? Anders Nordsten, aus Dänemark. Wir sind uns letzten Sonntag bei Frau Dennison's Haus begegnet."

"Oh yes, I mean *ja ja."* Loren remembered that Nordsten was on a grant from the Danish government to study American techniques for making European cheese. The next moment he remembered having seen that towering figure more recently than Sunday; just yesterday in fact, racing at top speed across the path of Wright's taxi. *"Ich habe Sie auch gestern gesehen,"* he said. *"Sie waren. . . . sehr schnell. . . ."* At the verb form he needed to convey the idea that the other had been running very fast Loren's seldom used German failed him and he fell back on pantomime, running in place with his arms swinging like a jogger. A woman at a table behind him laughed hysterically.

"Ja ja." Nordsten's face lit up in an incandescent smile. "I am in Denmark number three runner," he said in hesitant English. "In October go I to New York for Marathon. Twenty-six mile. *Jeden Nachmittag renne ich hier auf den Landwege."*

So he'd just been out on a practice run yesterday. Nothing sinister about that, Loren decided. At that moment he saw Wright coming out of the pickled-pine door marked MEN and with a sigh of relief began moving along the aisle again towards the cabbie's table.

"*Warum nicht essen mit mir?*" Nordsten asked.

"*Eine Moment, bitte,*" Loren said, and when he reached Wright's table, asked if he'd mind listening to two men converse in German over lunch.

"Mind? Why I'd be pleased!" Wright stood up and followed Loren to Nordsten's booth. "I was stationed in Berlin when I was an MP back in the Fifties. Picked up some of the language but I sure don't get much chance to use it here 'cept once in a while when a busload of German tourists hits town."

They scuttled into the booth opposite the Dane, Loren introduced the driver and when a waitress hovered over them a few minutes later they ordered: four-cheese chef salad for Loren, Gruyere cheeseburger and fries for Wright. Nordsten already had his meal in front of him, a pasta dish and, surprising for a marathon runner, a stein of dark beer. "Not same like which we drink in Denmark," he said, groping for the proper English words.

"Living overseas for two years spoiled me," Wright said in German that to Loren's ears was perfect. "Ever since I got out of the Army all American beer has tasted to me as if it were brewed inside a horse." Nordsten all but fell out of the booth laughing.

The waitress brought their lunches but Wright's fries went cold and limp and Loren picked absently at his greens as all of them swapped stories about Germany, Nordsten telling of races he had run, Wright reliving his soldiering days in a Berlin still in rubble from wartime bombing and not yet divided by the Wall, Loren telling of visits to the great university towns, combing through libraries and archives, hunting material for a legal history of the Third Reich that he'd worked on intermittently for years and finally abandoned as pointless. Whenever Nordsten had trouble with his English or Loren with his German, Wright carried them over the linguistic bridge.

They lingered in the dining area until every other table but theirs was empty and the waitress was beginning to frown at them. Loren looked at his watch and discovered with a shock that it was well after two. "We have to get going," he whispered to Wright.

"Right with you," the driver said, and reached into his pocket for a Call Me a Taxi business card which he handed to Nordsten with an invitation in German to phone for a ride whenever he had a destination he didn't feel like running to. Five minutes later Loren was in the cab again and headed for Vale.

It was after four when the station wagon turned in at Moxley's Auto Repair but the Camry wasn't quite ready yet. "Another half hour tops," the leaden-eyed mechanic on desk duty mumbled through a wad of bubble gum. Wright offered to wait around but Loren insisted he start back to Dennison and promised to call after supper. Stranded in a somnolent small town with nothing to read or do and nowhere to sit that wasn't spotted with grease or oil, he killed time with a walk to the other end of Vale and back.

Crossing Main Street opposite the body shop's front lot, he noticed a dark sedan with Wisconsin plates that hadn't been there when he'd set out. The car barely registered on his consciousness.

With his hand twisting the knob of the smeary glass door that led into the office area he happened to notice the two women standing at the stained counter talking with Leaden Eyes. One was short and thick-waisted with stiff gray hair, the other had soft white hair and the fragile look of a Dresden china doll. He froze. Then with infinite gentleness he released the doorknob and moved out of sight of the three people in the office, hoping desperately that none of them had seen him.

They were the ones. This was their car. Now that he looked at it closely he saw the FFF sticker on its rear bumper. He hadn't noticed it during Sunday morning's thunderous downpour when they had parked under the overpass on the opposite side of the highway from him and disabled his Camry with baseball bats, chanting "Damnation to detheifiers." Centuries ago their ancestors had probably helped the holy fathers of the Inquisition to stretch heretics on the rack or the reverend clergy of Salem to burn witches.

He slipped out of the lot, strolled casually down Main Street, crossed to the other side and entered a tavern with BEER in tired blue neon festooned in its front window. The place was empty except for the knot of bored old guzzlers who are found on the barstools of every small-town saloon. He ordered a draft beer, sauntered to the window table, set his schooner down untasted and peered past the neon tubing at Moxley's lot thirty yards down the deserted street.

Time seemed to stop. Loren would have guessed hours had gone by but his watch told him it was 5:04 when the old women came out of the body shop and got into the dark sedan and drove away. He would have bet a year's salary they would not drive far. Leaden Eyes would have told them the shop closed at six and they would count on Loren's returning to claim the Camry no later. He waited another five minutes, then trotted diagonally across Main and stepped into Moxley's office. This time the car was ready. So was the bill.

With a debit of several hundred dollars on his plastic he drove out of the lot, onto Main and, less than a block further, swung into the state highway. He kept the speed at a sedate fifty through a landscape of green tranquil hills, cows munching grass, silos and toy farmhouses in the distance. In the rear vision mirror he saw a black dot that stayed a quarter mile behind him. It could be them, it could be anyone.

As he approached the next turnoff he flicked his signal and slowed to thirty. Looping above the state road on the overpass he saw the dark sedan below signal and turn as he had. He swerved into the ramp on the opposite side of the highway and headed back towards Vale. Less than a minute later the black dot was centered in his rearview mirror again. *Good*, Loren thought.

He kept the Camry at fifty until he saw the answer to his hopes come up in his windshield, an unpaved farm road making a T with the highway. Dust clouds from the graveled track enveloped him the moment he made the turn. He slowed again to thirty. All he could see in the rearview mirror was brown particles swirling.

Then he saw it again, centered in the rectangle of mirror, the black dot dimly visible through the curtain of dirt.

Except for cows nothing alive was in sight along the farm road. Two miles from the highway he pumped the brake, slued the Camry in a K turn, hit the gas, aimed square at the dark sedan that grew larger in his windshield every second. The speed needle showed forty, forty-five, fifty.

The old ladies panicked first. He was twenty seconds at most from collision when they braked and began rocketing back towards the highway in reverse. They lasted a few hundred yards before the dark sedan spun off the gravel track and hung suspended with front wheels spinning and rear wheels sunk in the ditch.

Loren braked, cut his motor, stalked out and over to the dark impotently swaying sedan, tore open the driver's side door which the women like most Midwesterners had not troubled to lock. The terror in their eyes warmed him. He reached behind the driver's seat to the backseat floor and pulled out the two baseball bats, tossed one behind him, brandished the other.

"Turn off that motor!" he roared over the engine's anguished howl.

The blocky one with permed hair sat trembling spastically behind the wheel, unable to will her hand to move. Loren thrust his own hand in, wrenched the key from the ignition and stuffed it in his pocket.

"Get out," he ordered.

Both women sat motionless with eyes bulging. Loren's nostrils caught the smell of urine from the blocky one behind the wheel. He lifted the bat and ash wood cracked savagely against safety glass. When the windshield was a network of cracks he smashed the sedan's steering wheel and instrument panel. "Out!" he thundered at them, and stepped back a pace.

The permed woman squeezed her eyes shut in shame and fear and forced herself to sidle through the opening. The older-looking woman with the snowy hair stumbled out the passenger door and gave a high thin shriek as she fell into the ditch.

"Take off your shoes." Loren loomed over the permed woman like an avenging fury. She stood there frozen, tree-trunk legs spread apart. "Your shoes!" he screamed, and pushed her down onto the edge of the front seat and raised the bat to his shoulder.

Fear overcame paralysis. She bent over with a grunt and tugged off her low-heeled black shoes. Loren took them in one hand and tossed them into the Camry. Then he strode around the upraised front of the dark sedan to the white-haired woman sprawled in the ditch. "Yours too," he said.

Mumbling under her breath what Loren assumed was a prayer, the old woman handed him her shoes. He went around the dark sedan's hood and threw those into the Camry too. Then he came back and stood between the two terrified women.

"The next time you bitches come near me," he said, "I'll use this to break your legs. Clear?" They said nothing. "IS THAT CLEAR?" The white-haired woman nodded dumbly and the permed one managed to stutter a y-y-y-yes.

"And I know who sent you too," he added, making what he decided was a justified leap in the dark. "Tell that fat pig with the JSBACH license plate he's next." He moved back to where he could see into the sedan, scanned it for a cell phone, found none. "How you get out of here is your problem," he said. He scooped up the second bat, tossed both into the Camry and pulled away.

His heart pounded. For the time it took him to reach the T intersection with the state road he thought he was about to have a seizure. Then the pounding died and he was back on paved highway, skimming at fifty amid light traffic, going in the wrong direction but feeling more alive than he'd felt since the last time he and a woman he cared for had made love.

Thank you, Dad, for leaving me your vicious streak as well as your money, he said to himself. *Thank you, Lydia, for showing me the way.* As twilight blanketed the eastern sky he felt content, at peace, whole. But he kept the presence of mind to turn off at the first interchange beyond Vale that showed golden arches. He parked behind the McDonald's, waited until no customers were in sight, picked up the two pairs of shoes from the Camry's floor and dumped them in the waste can at the side of the building. Inside over coffee and a pastry he spread out the Wisconsin map from the door pocket and worked out a roundabout route back to Dennison. Then he filled up his tank at a service station with an automated car wash machine from which the Camry emerged shining wet and free of the farm road's dirt.

On unfamiliar roads and with a detour to toss the baseball bats in a convenient river, the return trip took longer than he expected. It was after seven and the clouds in the west were bathed in sunset glow when the Camry's stereo began picking up the signal from KDEN: the finale of Ralph Vaughan Williams' *London Symphony*, the haunting evocation of dusk descending on the Thames.

He had just passed a road sign DENNISON 7 when he heard the siren behind him. He threw a panicked glance at the speed readout but it was still locked at fifty. *Oh God, the old bitches hadn't found a state trooper, had they?* Blue and white roof-bar lights blazed in his rearview mirror. With cold fear in his stomach he pulled to the shoulder and braked. A uniformed trooper came out of the cruiser, approached the Camry and motioned Loren to lower the driver's side window. "Is your name Mensing, sir?" he asked politely.

"Yes," Loren croaked through dry lips, and began digging frantically in his trousers pocket for his wallet and license. "Officer, I wasn't . . ."

"There's been some trouble, sir. Captain Stacy, the chief of homicide in Dennison, put out a bulletin for all state patrol cars to keep an eye out for you."

"What kind of trouble?" Loren fought to keep unease out of his voice.

"He'll tell you, sir. You need to follow me." The trooper returned to his car and led the way with siren off and roof-bar lights still whirling. The route they took bypassed the business section but in the distance Loren made out the street-light glow of downtown. Finally they turned onto a road he recognized: Jeff Wright had used it driving him to the reception a little more than forty-eight hours ago. Fear roiled in Loren's belly.

First the state cruiser and then the Camry passed under the stone archway and along the approach road to the Dennison mansion. The paved area in front of the house was ablaze with light from portable floods, cluttered with Dennison police cars and crime scene unit vehicles and vans from TV stations. As Loren left the Camry and was being escorted up the steps by the trooper, a stocky rumpled figure came out by the front door, held it open and stood framed in the vestibule's light. Barney Lewis.

"Thanks, Officer," the prosecutor said. "I'll take over from here." The trooper nodded and took the steps two at a time back to his cruiser.

"Lewis," Loren demanded with the ice of dread congealing in him, "what the hell is going on here?"

"Another murder. With a club just like Phil Clift only different. They're taking the body out now, maybe you'd better not look."

Two white-coated technicians came out from around the side of the house, trundling between them a gurney with a figure shrouded head to toe in a rubber sheet. *They killed Heather,* a voice whispered inside Loren, and he felt his knees turn to water. The men in white stuffed the gurney in the rear of an orange-striped EMS vehicle parked at the edge of the grass and climbed into the cab. The ambulance roared away, siren keening into the night.

"We may make an arrest," Lewis added. "Stace is around back where it happened. He thinks there's enough evidence to hold her."

"Hold who?" Loren almost screamed at him.

"I hate to tell you this, Professor, but it looks like your girlfriend did it."

"Did *what?*" Instinct and common sense gave him the answer before he asked the question but he had to hear the words from another's mouth before he would accept it.

"Beat Lydia to death two or three hours ago," Lewis said.

EIGHT

Two hours later they let him see her.

Captain Stacy escorted him up the broad marble staircase and down a corridor bright with light from wall fixtures shaped like candles. A uniformed policewoman sat in a stack chair beside a white-painted door, reading a paperback romance novel. "She awake?" the homicide chief whispered, tugging at his trim beard.

"I don't know, sir. There hasn't been a sound from her in the last half hour."

"And before that?"

"I heard her crying, sir."

Stacy snorted his contempt but said nothing. "Officer, this is Professor Mensing. He's engaged to the lady in there and it's possible he's also going to be her attorney. He can stay with her as long as he wants."

"You mean like all night, sir?" The policewoman's lips formed an incredulous O.

"Yesterday Mrs. Dennison invited me to spend the rest of my visit at her house," Loren told them. "If you'll check with the housekeeper you'll find that Jeff Wright of Call Me a Taxi dropped my suitcase here this morning. It's a dark gray Samsonite and you probably found it in one of the guest bedrooms when you searched this floor. That is where I stay until someone with legal authority puts me out. When I'm through

145

talking with Heather, Captain, I expect to be shown my room."

"Do it," Stacy told the policewoman, and wheeled and marched away. Loren reached past her and twisted the door's brass knob.

It was a large high-ceilinged room thick with shadows, one tiny nightlight glowing low on one wall. Loren made out a pair of deep-cushioned armchairs, a dresser, a mirrored vanity, a portable TV on a marble stand, twin night tables flanking a queen-size bed. Heather sprawled on the bed in a fetal position, wrapped in a down comforter, breathing raggedly, her back to him and the door. He tiptoed across the thick carpet and pulled the padded vanity bench over to the edge of the bed. "Heather," he said softly, "I know you're awake. We need to talk." When he touched her shoulder it was rigid as a board. He reached under the comforter to stroke her hands and felt them clammy with fear.

"Loren, don't." He could barely hear the words that dribbled from between her pale lips. "Please don't—try to con—console me. I don't deserve it. I'm—responsible. I killed her."

His hand froze on hers as if they had been grafted together beneath the comforter. This woman had committed a brutal murder and he as her lawyer was ethically bound to get her off by any of the abundant means defense counsel were offered by the system. The quicksand of his worst nightmare sucked at him. *I will not do that!* he cried out silently.

"I came here and first Mr. Clift was beaten to death and now Lydia . . . It's because of me," she sobbed. "This is my punishment. Oh God, please someone forgive me."

Fury gave Loren the strength to rip his hand from hers. He sprang up, kicked away the vanity bench and paced the open space of the bedroom, pounding his right fist into his left palm until the impulse to slap her was under control. Then he came back, bent over her, pulled off the comforter, made her sit, hooked the bench with his foot and dragged it back to the bedside.

"Now you listen to me." He kept his voice low so no one outside the door could hear but harsh so she would feel the anger burning in him. He felt his heart pounding, a band of pain in his chest. When she slumped forward like a rag doll he seized her shoulders and squeezed them savagely. "Look at me and listen to me, you damn fool! Whatever religious guilt you feel over what happened tonight may put you in prison, so stuff it! You will answer my questions in ordinary this-world language. Understood?"

She bobbed her head in a robot parody of assent, her eyes vacant as if she had retreated into a cavern deep within herself.

"Did you kill Lydia?"

She sat motionless. He wondered if she had heard him.

"If you did," he said, "and you tell me now, I will walk out of this room, tell Lewis I'm not representing you and let him convict you if he can. If you did and you don't tell me now and I find out later that you're guilty, I will do everything in my power to help him put you away for the rest of your life and I don't give a damn if I get disbarred for it. Now. Did you kill her?"

"N—n—no," she mumbled through trembling lips.

He relaxed his grip on her shoulders, felt the congestion in his chest ease off. "All right," he said. "Let's talk."

They sat in the matching armchairs with a mahogany drum table between them and he handed her a sheet of cardboard on which he had drawn a rough diagram of the basement and pool area after Lewis had briefed him.

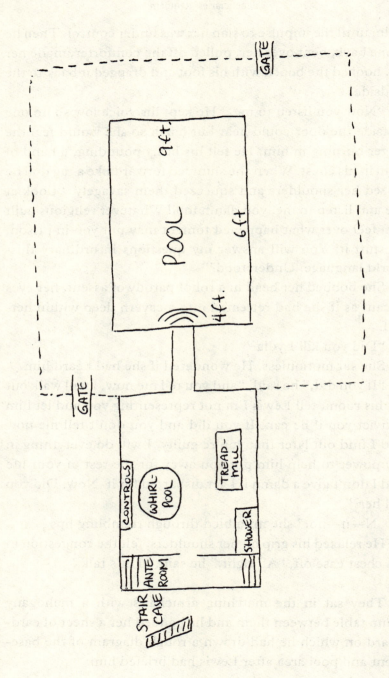

"How much do you know about what happened?" he asked. "Did Stacy or Lewis tell you any of it?"

"No, noth—nothing. I—found her naked in a pool of blood on the treadmill and I found her pager in the pocket of her robe and Fraser ran over from his apartment and looked at her and we called 911."

"What time did you find her?"

"I don't know, somewhere around six. She'd gone down for her daily routine at 4:30 and I began to worry when she didn't come up again."

"Can you handle hearing about it?"

"I've seen savagely abused women at the shelter and other women at the morgue who were beaten to death. This is different somehow, it's—it always feels as if part of me has been broken but this is the first time I don't feel I'll ever heal."

"I know," he said. "I didn't get to know her well but she was very dear to me too."

Heather sat up straighter in her chair and folded her arms against her breast as if she were cold. "Tell me how she died," she said.

By the time Lewis had taken Loren around as much of the basement and pool area as possible without risk of contaminating evidence, Fraser and the housekeeper had been interviewed by Stacy and the Crime Scene Unit people had found enough evidence to make a coherent picture. Lydia Dennison's exercise regimen never varied. "The German in her," Stacy had said. She would come down the stairs to the basement wearing sweats, gym socks and sneakers, an old robe in whose pocket she kept the pager that would summon Fraser in case of emergency. From the shelves built into the anteroom at the foot of the staircase she would select an audiocassette. Then she would hang her robe on a wall hook, insert the cassette into a battery-powered tape player attached to the treadmill's handrail by a loop of plastic-coated wire, plug the treadmill into the wall outlet, set the controls for mileage, rate and time, adjust the earphones and step aboard the moving belt. She would stay on the machine for somewhere between thirty and forty minutes: first a warm-up period, then fifteen minutes or more at 4.5 miles per hour, then a cool-down phase during which by slow stages she would reduce the rate to 3.0. Shutting off the machine, she would shuck her exercise clothes and jump into the shower she had had installed in the basement. When it was not too cold or raining she would finish by going out the door to the pool yard and swimming laps for twenty to thirty minutes. Then she would return to the basement, adjust the controls on the whirlpool and soak herself in scalding bubbling water for a quarter hour.

"I remember about three years ago the noon news program on one of the local TV stations was doing a series on fitness for seniors," Lewis had said. "They had a camera crew out here and she went through the whole routine for them only that time she wore a bathing suit in the pool. I happened to be down with the flu the day it ran and caught it on the tube. Interviewing Fraser and the housekeeper brought it all back to me. Christ, why do the good ones have to eat all the shit?"

After her soak she would throw on her old robe and a pair of thongs and pad back upstairs to her bedroom suite for a nap. Afterwards would come a drink, supper, an old Western in the video room with herself as the female lead, a gala social evening with fellow chamber music buffs or local luminaries, whatever. Sweat-encrusted gym outfit, the robe hanging on its wall hook, the treadmill still plugged into the wall, the moist cake of pink soap in the niche in the shower wall and the damp condition of the stall floor showed that she had followed the usual routine this afternoon. Until the murderer had interrupted her.

Loren had stood in the exercise room doorway with Barney Lewis while evidence technicians measured and dusted and scraped and recorded the scene with video cameras. His eyes scanned the cassettes arranged alphabetically two tiers to a shelf on the anteroom's built-in cabinet. Most of it was music for full orchestra: Beethoven, Brahms and Bruckner on the highest tier, Tchaikovsky and Ralph Vaughan Williams and the majestic organ symphonies of Louis Vierne on the lowest. "Around twenty minutes to five the housekeeper heard the treadmill go on," the prosecutor said. "She was finishing up in the kitchen, right over our heads."

"She could hear the machine through this thick ceiling?" Loren wondered.

"Jimson!" Lewis shouted across the room to a Crime Scene Unit man who was scraping a stain from the treadmill. "Turn on the gizmo a few seconds, will you?"

The gloved technician stooped over and depressed a button near floor level. Instantly the room was flooded by a rackety clanking din. "Yeah, she could hear that through the ceiling. We checked. Jimson, turn it off!" Lewis roared. No wonder, Loren thought, that Lydia preferred the overpowering type of classical music while she was on the treadmill. Nothing less could drown that machinery.

There was no way of telling precisely how long she had walked today, Lewis explained, because when the user hit the Stop button on that model of treadmill the timing clock continued to run. "But the distance clock does stop so we know just how far she went. Three miles even. So if she started at 4:40 she probably turned it off around 5:20. Then she would have stripped, showered, gone through that door to the pool and dived in."

"But no one actually saw her in the pool?"

"Professor, you've seen the privacy fence around the pool yard. That fence is eight feet high. Even from the loft apartments that used to be the coach house you can't see over into the pool. You get a view of it from some of the windows inside this house of course but no one was here after five o'clock but Heather and she says she didn't look."

"Then how do you know Lydia swam?" The moment the question was out of his mouth and beyond recall Loren cursed his idiocy.

"How the fuck do you think we know?" Lewis snorted. "Because she was still soaking wet from the chlorinated water when she got clubbed to death."

The two of them had left the house by the front door and walked out into the mild starry night with moonglow bathing the countryside under winking stars, vans with the call letters of TV stations on their sides dotting the front parking area, distant bushes alive with the songs of toads. That was when the sensation began to nag at Loren like the slow drip of water from a faucet. Either something was there in the exercise room that shouldn't have been or something was not there that should have been. Maybe both. He was still too numb from the shock of the murder to be able to think straight. It was an itch he couldn't scratch because he couldn't reach the part of him that was itching.

As reporters trained videocams on them and shouted questions they pretended they hadn't heard, Loren followed the prosecutor along the line of the privacy fence. They turned a corner guarded by uniforms who kept the TV crews at bay, made another right-angle turn and came to a gate in the fence on the side behind the pool. Lewis rammed with his shoulder. The gate didn't budge. "You want to try?" he invited. When Loren declined, the district attorney shouted over the top of the fence for one of the CSU team working the pool yard to unlatch for them. Inside the enclosure Loren examined the latch under one of the Department's portable floodlights. It was screwed into the red cedar boards at eye level, almost six feet from the ground.

"Anybody inside the pool yard who wants out, it's easy," Lewis pointed out as if Loren were the fool his last question had made him seem. "You lift the latch and walk through. When you shut the gate the latch relocks behind you. Anybody outside who wants in, you'd have to be a giraffe with hands. The gate on the other side of the house is built exactly the same."

"Suppose I was outside and wanted in and brought a stepladder with me," Loren suggested. "Why couldn't I lean it against the outside of the gate, climb up a few rungs, reach over and unlatch?"

"I suppose you could," Lewis conceded, frowning.

"In fact, if I knew where the latch was located, I could probably lift it with a coat hanger," Loren said.

As they traversed the pool area the prosecutor drew the murder scene so vividly Loren shivered. Lydia swimming laps in blissful inattention. The murderer emerging into the pool yard, either from the basement door or one of the gates in the fence, and waiting with weapon in hand for her to clamber out of the water. Then he springs at her, slams his club against the back of her neck. She falls hard on her knees, both of which were badly bruised from the concrete apron surrounding the pool. He looms over her, clubbing her again and again, on her head, her back and shoulders. If she cried out, no one heard. Somehow she manages to make it to her feet under the rain of blows. Naked and bloody she stumbles in unspeakable terror towards the basement door, desperate to get inside, reach her robe hanging on the wall hook near the shower stall, press the panic button of her pager in the robe's pocket. She flings the door open, gropes her way blindly into the exercise room with blood in her hair and eyes and the murderer a few steps behind her. She slips on the cold floor, falls against the treadmill. It is there that he crushes in that magnificent old woman's skull with blow after savage blow until the job is done. And then he leaves. Maybe through the gate in the fence and away, maybe upstairs and no further than the main floor of the house. While he reconstructed the crime Lewis had been walking Loren through the center of the exercise room, along a narrow path bordered by yellow crime scene tape, and they were back in the shelf-lined anteroom by the time he had finished.

"Whichever way the killer left," the prosecutor said, "he or she left the weapon behind." He pointed to a long tubular chalk mark on the exercise room floor. "Right there. You'll remember that Phil Clift's killer took his or her weapon away and dumped it in the park later. Now I wonder if you can guess what sort of bludgeon this murderer used."

A baseball bat like the pious ladies of the FFF? Another tire iron or crowbar? There were too many possibilities and, having no basis for winnowing them down, Loren said nothing.

"It was your girlfriend's cane beat Lydia to death," Lewis said.

Loren felt tightness gripping his chest and a sense of wild panic flooding through him. He stumbled back a few steps, seized the handrail of the basement stairs for support. "You all right?" Lewis asked. "You need a medic?"

"Give me a minute," Loren gasped. He lowered himself to one of the bottom steps and sat hunched over, taking deep breaths. When his heartbeat seemed normal again he looked up with a moronic vacant stare. "You're—sure her cane did it?"

"It's at the lab now. There was blood all over it plus smears we think came from the chlorinated water in the pool. Lydia's hair was sopping wet when she was clubbed."

"That's impossible," Loren said.

"What's impossible?" Lewis growled. "Cops found the cane exactly where you see that chalk mark. We have it on videotape."

"Heather couldn't have . . . My God, she had no reason to kill Lydia, she loved her! If she committed the murder why didn't she take the cane with her when she left the basement? Why did she come down again and call Fraser and 911?"

"Maybe we'll have answers to those questions tomorrow," Lewis said.

"Look." Loren gripped the handrail and hoisted himself to his feet. "Heather was attacked just last week by someone whose weapon of choice is also a club. Her knee was injured. She can't walk without that cane."

"If it was Heather who attacked Lydia outside with the cane," Lewis pointed out, "and her knee gave on her and she fell down, that might explain how Lydia managed to make it back inside the house."

"If Lydia was killed with Heather's cane and Heather didn't do it, she must have some explanation how she and the cane got—well, separated. You've talked with her and I haven't. Does she?"

"Stacy talked with her, not me. Hey, Stace!" he called across the basement room. "Got a second?"

The trim-bearded homicide chief was holding a cell phone to his ear and huddling with two of his investigators. He handed the phone to one of them and came over to the ante-room along the tape-bordered pathway through the exercise room's center. "Something's just come up," he told Lewis. "I'm going to have to leave for a while."

"This'll just take a minute. Professor Mensing here wants to know what Ms. Dennison said about how come her cane wound up down here. I don't see any harm in telling him and in fact I'd like to hear the story myself."

"She wasn't all that coherent when I questioned her," Stacy replied, "but she claims she left the cane down here early this afternoon. Lydia had her in the whirlpool soaking her bad knee and then she rubbed some salve on it and covered it with a fresh bandage. It felt so much better she thought she'd try getting around without the cane for a while. So she says."

"The housekeeper was here till five," Loren pointed out. "What does she say?"

"She backs up that part of the story," Stacy admitted. "Saw her walking around the house, limping a little but getting by okay."

"Doesn't mean squat," Lewis cut in. "She could still have come down later, retrieved the cane, gone through that door to the pool area and done the murder. In fact, Professor, when you stop to think, who else could possibly have done it? No one knew the cane was down here except Lydia herself and the old housekeeper."

"All right," Loren said. "Let's forget that Heather was a victim too. Let's forget she had no motive to kill Lydia. Do you really think she's so stupid she'd commit this murder in a way that would point to her so blatantly?"

"She would if subconsciously she wanted us to pin it on her," Stacy said. "No one has ever really understood the mind of a murderer except maybe Dostoevsky." That was the moment when an insight seized Loren. This dainty little detective saw himself as Porfiry Petrovich in *Crime and Pun-*

ishment and Heather as his Raskolnikov.

"If you'd like to see her now," Stacy said as he adjusted the folds of his red scarf about his throat, "I'll take you."

By the time Loren finished telling her she was weeping softly. He saw a box of tissues on the dresser top and brought them to her.

"They really believe—I could do something so—so horrible," she said. "When I've spent years working eighteen-hour days at the shelter to save women from being beaten and abused and . . ."

"Try to see it from their perspective," Loren told her. "You and Lydia were all but enclosed in a sealed environment when it happened, just the two of you. No outsider could get into the house without setting off the alarm. Into the pool yard, well, maybe but it's not very likely. So you seem to be the only person who had opportunity, and your cane was the weapon. I'll tell you frankly, you're lucky they haven't already arrested you."

"But, Loren, I had no motive!" It was a cry of desperation like the scream of a small animal whose leg is being chewed by a hunter's trap. "I am a . . ." Before she could finish the sentence Loren touched his palm to her lips while his other hand gestured to the corridor door with the unseen police-woman on its far side.

"They'll know you're a nun soon enough," he said just loud enough for her to hear. "This murder was made to order for the media. Vans from network affiliates in Madison and Milwaukee pulled into the front yard while I was with Lewis. CNN can't be far behind. By the time Domjan wakes up in New York tomorrow this story will be on the morning news and he'll be on the phone to Lewis spilling your little secret. That's if Lewis doesn't call him first. I came close to telling the story myself but decided it would sound better coming from you. For your own good I advise you to go down and give him everything as soon as you've pulled yourself together."

"Yes, you're right, of course you're right. Then they'll know I couldn't have done this."

"Don't delude yourself," Loren said. "You can't tell the whole story without telling about your—what's the word for it, faith crisis? That's going to be catnip for the media too. You're going to have your fifteen minutes of fame whether you like it or not. The religious zealots out there will call you a traitor and a pariah and say if you're degraded enough to doubt God's word you're degraded enough to commit a brutal murder. Except those who are anti-Catholic, and they're going to think of you as a nun and lump you with all the priests who've been exposed as child molesters. The people who've seen through religion—who knows what they'll think? Heather, you're in a terrible hole and you've put me in it with you."

"Loren, I swear I never meant—I was only trying to help . . ."

He took the mess of soggy tissues from her lap, tossed them in a gilded wastebasket and held her hand in his own. "I know you intended no harm," he said. "And every instinct I have tells me you didn't commit this murder. That means someone else did. And the only other suspect we have is Alec."

"But that makes no sense either!" she insisted.

"Why doesn't it?" *Her mind is engaged again,* Loren thought. *Good.*

She shut her tear-moist eyes and said nothing for a minute, then opened them and leaned forward in her arm-chair. "Because—this is assuming he exists at all—however many other murders he committed, he did them to get more

158

money out of the trust for himself or someone very close to him. But Lydia's trust income was completely independent. Whatever happened to the rest of the beneficiaries, she always got half, no more and no less."

"Now that she's dead the trust terminates," Loren said. "What happens to the half of the principal that generated her half of the income?"

Heather chewed on her lower lip, trying to remember. "Uncle Almon's trust gave her a testamentary power of appointment over it," she answered then. "It goes wherever her will says it goes. To the Cultural Foundation, I suppose, to support classical music. That's the only cause she cared about."

"Is that what she told you? Did she show you her will?"

"No, of course not, what business was it of mine?"

"Remember what you learned in my Estates course? The holder of a power of appointment is under no legal obligation to exercise it. We don't know for sure that Lydia did, do we? Let's suppose for a moment that she didn't, where does the principal that generated her half of the income go now that she's dead?"

"Loren, I don't know! I can't even remember if there's a provision in the trust instrument that covers that possibility! Where's the copy of the will I made for you?"

"In my attaché case," he said, "in the trunk of my car. I'm not going outside to get it with all those TV crews in the front yard."

"But if there were a provision saying if she didn't exercise her power then half the principal would go to some named person or persons when she died—one of us would remember that, wouldn't we?"

"I certainly would if the named person were one of the other beneficiaries," Loren said, "because that would have lifted him or her to the status of relative most likely to be Alec."

"But . . ." She pulled her hand from Loren's and clenched her fists in a frenzy of frustration. "The Cultural Foundation, the Chamber Ensemble, all the trust properties—the only beneficiary who had anything to do with any of them was Phil Clift and he was killed Sunday night! I simply can't see how Alec, whoever he is, could profit from killing however many other beneficiaries he's murdered and also profit from killing Lydia!"

"That's it in a nutshell," Loren told her. "You've just put your finger on the biggest puzzle that confronts us. If I can ever find the answer, I'll have this thing licked." He took off his glasses, rubbed his aching eyes. When he replaced the glasses all he could see was blurs. If only he could put his finger with the same precision on what was disturbing him about the basement exercise room, the thing that was there but shouldn't have been, or that wasn't there but should. "I'm too beat to think about it anymore tonight," he said, stifling a cavernous yawn, and the next moment found himself fighting to suppress a rueful laugh. "I'm so damn tired I forgot I've had nothing to eat since lunch."

"Me neither. Remember, we were holding supper till you came back with your car. Lydia chilled a bottle of Johannisberger Riesling and whipped up a crab salad. The thought of eating it now makes me sick."

"Me too," Loren said. He brought his wristwatch up to his good eye. Almost eleven-thirty. "Let's find Lewis. I'll stay with you while you're telling him about yourself. Then I'm going to take some valium and give you a couple too. Tomorrow's apt to be miserable for both of us and we need sleep while we can get it." Hand in hand they trudged along the corridor to the head of the main staircase. As they were starting down the curving marble steps, Captain Stacy and the two plainclothesmen who had been with him in the basement started up. When the homicide chief saw Loren and Heather descending he and his detectives retreated to the foot of the stairs and waited for them.

"I thought you had to go somewhere," Loren said.

"Didn't take long. Turned out worthwhile."

"We have something we want to say to Barney Lewis," Loren told him.

"Barney had to go out too," Stacy said. "To Dennison Memorial. His father saw the story about the murder on the late news and had a coronary."

"Oh dear God, no," Heather whispered. Her already pale face went fish-belly gray and she clutched the material of Loren's jacket like a life raft.

"My errand was different." With a nod to his men Stacy took a step forward and blocked her way. "Heather Dennison," he said, "I arrest you for the murder of Lydia Dennison. You have the right to remain silent. You have the right to be represented by an attorney. If you cannot afford an attorney one will be appointed for you. You are coming with us right now."

Loren was too stunned to react. He felt Heather's body go limp as if she were about to fall over. One of the detectives disengaged her hand from Loren's jacket as the other produced a pair of handcuffs.

"Mr. Mensing," Stacy said, "you can't go to Headquarters with us and you're not welcome here any more. You have five minutes to get your bag and leave this house."

NINE

Heather was cuffed and clinging numbly to Loren's hand, her eyes unfocused and glassy. All that came from between her lips was "I didn't . . . I didn't . . ." At Stacy's nod the bulky plainclothesmen pried her fingers from Loren's hand, each man gripping her above one elbow, dragged her slowly backwards to the front door. "Loren, please . . ." The door slammed shut and cut her off. Stacy punched the code in the security panel that would keep the burglar alarm from sounding, then came back to where Loren stood stunned at the foot of the stairs.

"We won't question her till tomorrow," he said. "If you're representing her you have the right to be present, if you're not you have no rights at all. It's up to you to check in with me in the morning and tell me where you stand."

"What gives you the right to evict me from this house?" Loren demanded.

"As far as I'm concerned the whole place is a crime scene. We need to secure it till we get a warrant tomorrow, search her room, her belongings, the works. You're supposed to be her fiancé. That means maybe you'd be tempted to fuck around with evidence if I let you stay."

Loren was still too disoriented to think straight. "I need to make some phone calls before I go," he said.

"Find a 7-11 and make 'em there." A uniform trudged down the stairs carrying Loren's Samsonite suitcase.

"There's your bag," Stacy snapped. "If you're not gone in two minutes I'll arrest you for obstruction of justice. Out."

Loren slammed the trunk lid, climbed into the driver's seat, thrust his key in the ignition. A knot of reporters and minicam operators came trotting towards the Camry from their vans. With his heart like a drumbeat he roared up the long drive to the stone archway, brakes screaming as he made the turn. He tried to calm himself, concentrate on the sheet of light his highway beams threw on the dark silent road, locate a landmark somewhere in the empty night. Five minutes' driving and he was lost. He blundered along two-lane roads, not knowing if he was headed for town or into the vast countryside, desperate for a road sign that would orient him. Nothing. It was as if he were the last living creature on earth.

Then at the foot of a hill where two roads intersected he saw a low square structure surrounded by arc lights and aimed for it. The service station was closed but there was a pay phone on a concrete post at the corner of the lot. He fumbled in his wallet for the Call Me a Taxi card, fed a quarter into the slot and stabbed numbers. One ring, two, three, four . . . *Answer, please for God's sake answer!* he begged the silence.

"Wright residence." There were undertones of sleepiness, anger and fear but it was unmistakably the voice of Jefferson Wright. Loren guessed that calls to the business number were forwarded to the home number after a certain hour.

"It's Loren Mensing . . ."

That was as far as he got. "Oh, my Lord, it's you!" the driver exclaimed. "Jessie and me we heard on the TV news about what happened to Miss Lydia and we been phoning and phoning her house and getting busy signals."

"You won't hear the latest news till morning," Loren said.

163

"They kicked me out and arrested Heather for murder. She's innocent." He paused, tried to collect his thoughts, then rolled the dice. "Could I ask you for two favors? One's small and the other's huge."

"Better start with the small one," Wright suggested cautiously.

"I'm calling from a service station. Hang on a second." He left the handset dangling on its cord, ran to the front of the dark blocky building and straight back. "I'm at the pay phone at Oscar's Citgo, it's closed for the night. Can you tell me how I get from here to Dennison Memorial Hospital?"

He found a pen in his jacket and the invoice from Moxley's Auto Repair in his wallet and scrawled on the back of the bill the directions Wright dictated. "Thanks," he said.

"No trouble. Now what's the huge favor?"

"Well . . ." Loren hesitated, uncertain how to ask, knowing that if their positions were reversed, if someone he had met only a few days before were to wake him up this late and make the request Loren was trying to find words for, his answer would almost certainly be No. "I need a place to stay where the media won't find me," he said then. "How much would it take to persuade you to turn your house into, well, sort of a bed and breakfast for a few days?"

"What you planning to do with the few days?"

"Find out who really killed Lydia. Save Heather if I can. I don't have much time, she's already starting to come apart over this."

"You sure she didn't do it?"

"Things look bad for her," Loren said. "Maybe worse than I know. That's why I have to go to the hospital first. So I can't honestly tell you I'm sure she didn't do it. I don't think she did. If I find out she did I'll do everything I can to nail her for it. I'm asking you to just assume she's innocent till we know more and help me find the real murderer before she cracks. Please."

The other end of the line was silent. Loren held the handset in a strangler's grip, waiting. The hammering of his heart felt like thunderclaps.

"You know," Wright said at last, "Miss Lydia paid me a thousand dollars to drive you around and see to you till your car was ready. Seems to me I ain't truly earned that much yet." As Loren groped for the auto repair bill and his pen Wright gave directions from the hospital to his house. "Jessie and me have a spare room for when the grandkids visit. You sure are lucky ain't none visitin' right now."

"I—don't have the words to thank you for this," Loren said.

"You don't need them. We'll wait up for you."

Dennison Memorial Hospital was a tan brick complex at the edge of the business district, three stories tall, bathed in sodium vapor lights, connected by a covered walkway with a 24-hour parking structure. Loren eased into a vacant slot, made sure all the Camry's doors were locked and took the walkway at a lope. An electric eye slid back double glass doors at the far end of the ramp and a beefy security guard in blue uniform rose from a stool and blocked his path. "Help you, sir?" he asked politely.

"I'm Professor Mensing." Loren produced his driver's license and law school ID card. "You know about the murder at Mrs. Dennison's house?" Before the guard could reply Loren went on. "I'm working on the case with your district attorney, Barney Lewis. Something's happened that I need to see him about right away. I understand he's here, his father had a heart seizure when he heard about the murder. Miles Lewis?"

"Let me check for you, sir." The guard took a walkie-talkie from his leather belt and, when he heard it squawking, spoke softly into the mouthpiece. "Mr. Lewis is waiting in the third floor lounge," he reported after a muffled conversation. "Elevator's halfway down this hall. Press three," he added, as if Loren were retarded. "You'll see a nurses' station when you step out, somebody there will show you to the lounge."

He rose one flight in a cold steel box three times larger than a regular elevator. A bone-thin woman in crisp whites led him along dim hushed passages smelling of disinfectant and fear. Through half-open doorways he glimpsed huddled forms in stiff comfortless beds, heard snores and prayers and soft moans of pain. The nurse tapped lightly on a closed door marked PRIVATE, opened it and shepherded Loren around nests of cushioned chairs and low pine tables to the bank of windows where Barney Lewis paced against a backdrop of star-flecked darkness. "This gentleman says you'd want to see him," she said dubiously.

"Yeah, it's okay, thanks." The prosecutor sank onto a lumpy couch and motioned Loren to join him.

"How's your father doing?" Loren asked.

"He's ninety years old and his ticker's never been all that great, how do you think he's doing?" Lewis growled. "I'm sorry," he said then. "One thing and another, this has been my worst day in a hell of a long while. His doctor's supposed to come by and give me the prognosis, then I have to go home and catch a little sleep. You didn't come here to ask me about Pop."

"I came to ask you why Stacy took Heather to jail. I can't believe he did that behind your back."

"We talked about it over the phone before he arrested her," Lewis admitted.

"Would you mind telling me why he did it?" Loren fought

166

to keep his voice a hospital whisper.

"Remember he got a call just before you and I talked with him in Lydia's basement? That call was from Everett Marshall. Know who he is?"

"I've never heard the name in my life," Loren said.

"Yeah, that's right, he was out of town Sunday and couldn't make it to the reception so maybe you haven't met him. Everett Marshall was Lydia's personal attorney. When he heard the top story on the ten o'clock TV news he drove down to the PD to report something he was afraid might be connected with the murder. Lydia made an appointment and went to see him Monday afternoon. Like to try guessing what for?"

Loren sat rigid. One of his eyelids twitched.

"Almon Dennison's will gave Lydia power of appointment over the fifty percent of the trust principal that generated her share of the income but she had to exercise that power in her own will. Ever since she became a widow, her will provided when she died that money was to go to the Cultural Foundation to support classical music activities in Dennison. It was never a secret that's the way she'd exercised her power. Then less than forty-eight hours ago she tells Marshall she's changed her mind. Like to try guessing who the new lucky person is?"

Loren said nothing. He felt weak, as if the blood were being drained from him.

"Back at the house we were stuck on what reason she would have had to kill Lydia," Lewis said. "Now we know. That's why Stacy arrested her."

Stupid, stupid! Loren cursed himself. If only he had understood the hints Lydia had dropped during her Monday morning conversation with him at the Cheese Country Inn, if he had asked her point blank that afternoon about her mysterious business downtown, maybe he and Heather could have prevailed on her to tear up the codicil, go back to the way she had originally exercised her power of appointment. Maybe they could have saved her life. Or had Heather known about the codicil all along? Might she have influenced Lydia to execute it in the first place? Had Loren been duped from the beginning by a brutal and cold-blooded murderess who also happened to be a nun?

"Marshall brought a xerox of the codicil to the PD and they faxed a copy to my office." Lewis groped in his jacket pocket and pulled out two pages of thin crinkly paper. "Here, read it and weep."

Loren switched on a table lamp next to his seat on the couch and scanned the pages as a rising sense of panic filled him. CODICIL TO MY LAST WILL AND TESTAMENT. Standard introductory legal jargon, then the crux of the document. "The power of appointment conferred upon me under the will of my late husband Almon Dennison, dated April 17, 1952, I hereby exercise as follows. I direct that upon my death the amount of the principal of the trust created under the said will of my late husband Almon Dennison and made subject to my power of appointment by the terms of said will shall be paid to my beloved grandniece Heather Dennison, currently residing at 235 West 71st Street, New York, N.Y. 10023. It is my wish that this money be used for the continuation of the work of the New York Shelter for Battered Women and Children, with which my grandniece has worked for the past several years." More legal jargon, Lydia's signature, the signatures of the required two witnesses, Monday's date.

"As a professor of trusts and estates," Lewis said, "you'll appreciate the precatory language. Heather's not under any legal obligation to use the money for the shelter. She could move to the Riviera and live the sweet life on it if the fancy struck her. That's assuming we don't convict her of murder of course."

"Heather wouldn't do that," Loren insisted doggedly, no longer sure he believed his own words. "Her life is other people. She is as close to a selfless person as I've ever met."

"Then how come Lydia didn't leave her the money in trust, put her under an enforceable duty to use it for the shelter?"

"If I had to guess I'd say that Lydia—well, loved and trusted Heather totally. Knew that she wouldn't spend the money on herself. Putting her under a trustee's fiduciary obligations would have been an insult. What does Marshall say Lydia told her?"

"Something like that," Lewis admitted. "She said that getting to know Heather, getting close to her, she'd decided classical music wasn't as important as helping the helpless. She also told him she was planning to cut back on her annual contributions to the Cultural Foundation and give that money to the shelter too."

"Did Marshall tell anyone else about this conversation?"

"A confidential communication between attorney and client? Come on, Professor, haven't you heard of legal ethics?"

"Well then Lydia did," Loren insisted. "Because Dan Feinberg expected drastic funding cuts before she was murdered." Leaning forward on the hard stained cushions, he recounted the bizarre conversation he'd had with Feinberg at the Cultural Foundation office Tuesday morning. "And if she told Feinberg she probably told others too, or else he did. Like Ward Dennison at the bank. Maybe Ellis Carr at KDEN. Ask around and I bet you'll find most of the inner circle in this town knew about that codicil before the ink was dry on Lydia's signature."

"Okay, let's assume they did," Lewis said. "The damage was already done by then, right? So how does that give anybody else either a motive to kill Lydia or opportunity or access to the murder weapon?"

"Let's put opportunity and access aside for a while," Loren urged. "Don't you see that if Lydia were killed *and Heather were convicted for it* any interested party could bring a civil action to have the codicil set aside? Remember the old one-liner from common law: No one is allowed to profit from their own crime."

Lewis rubbed his stubbly jaw as if his skin were irritating him. "So you're saying if another party knew about the codicil and decided to kill Lydia and frame Heather . . ."

"That would answer your question about motive. And if this same party had been increasing his or her own share of the trust over the years by systematically killing off other Dennison beneficiaries, including Phil Clift just last Sunday . . ."

"Alec again," Lewis said softly.

"It has to be," Loren argued. "Believe whatever you want to about Heather but at the time Phil Clift was killed she and I were the guests of honor at Lydia's reception, under the eyes of two hundred people including yourself!"

"Oh, of course she didn't do Clift. But maybe the setup gave her the idea for killing Lydia more or less the same way."

"But that brings us back to what I asked you a few hours ago. How could this female Iago you've made up out of whole cloth be such an idiot she'd commit a murder that pointed so blatantly to herself?"

"How could anyone except Heather have committed the murder at all?" Lewis countered.

Loren was about to tell Lewis that the woman he'd allowed to be locked up was a nun when he realized he might hold one other card in his hand. "I think you can help me answer that question," he said. "Out at the house you told me a local TV station did a segment on Lydia's fitness routine a few years ago."

"They did," Lewis said. "I saw it on the tube myself."

"When a TV news crew does a piece on a local celebrity," Loren said, "it's usually not trashed after it's broadcast. The station files it for possible use in the future. Remember, Lydia was already well into her seventies when the exercise segment was shot. The station managers must have known that within the next few years they'd need footage for her obituary story. So chances are the video footage is still in their archives."

"And if it is?"

"I want to see it," Loren said. "Everything they shot and still have, even outtakes. I'd like you to call the station in the morning and ask them to make you a copy." He twisted on the couch and leaned forward intensely. "Something I saw down in that basement was wrong. I know it but I can't put my finger on it. If I see Lydia go through her exercise routine maybe I can. Will you do that for me?"

For what seemed to Loren like an hour the prosecutor sat unmoving in the darkened lounge. "Here's how I see it," he said then. "We're sort of on opposite sides in this thing and also sort of not. I won't prosecute someone unless I'm dead certain they're guilty and you won't defend someone unless you're dead certain they're innocent. Right now I'm *almost* dead certain your girlfriend's guilty."

Loren was about to play the last card in his hand, tell Lewis for whatever impact it might have that Heather was not his girlfriend but a nun, when the lounge door opened and a bald compact man in bifocals and surgical greens threaded his way through the clusters of chairs and couches to the bank of windows. The district attorney lumbered to his feet and Loren mechanically rose too.

"We've stabilized him," the doctor said. "He's out of immediate danger but we'll need to keep him here a few days, do some tests. You and your friend might as well go home. You both look like you need to sleep a week."

"Thanks, doc." Lewis wrung the heart surgeon's hand. "I'll call you in the morning."

"I'll see you in the morning too," Loren promised. "Not early. Will you please get that video footage for me?"

"Yeah," Lewis said.

TEN

He came slowly out of valium sleep, groped for the glasses he had left on the bedside table atop his copy of Almon Dennison's trust and some scratch paper, and opened his eyes to discover with a start that the room was bright with sunlight and according to the battery clock on the pine-paneled wall amid framed photographs of black athletes and pop stars it was almost ten. Finding the Wrights' modest frame house, stowing the Camry in their garage and telling them as much as he dared of the inside story behind Lydia Dennison's murder had kept him from bed till after two A.M., and rereading portions of the trust instrument while he waited for the valium to put him under had kept him awake till close to three. In robe and pajamas he cracked open the spare bedroom's door and slithered down a corridor barely wider than himself to the bathroom. By 10:15 he was showered, shaved, dressed and sitting at the butcher-block table in the breakfast nook with his pills, a large glass of orange juice, a mug of steaming coffee and a plate of fresh blueberry muffins in front of him. The Wrights had already eaten and Jeff had gone out to fill the station wagon's tank and run some errands. Jessie, gray-haired and comfortably curved in a flow-ered print dress, sat across the table with her head cocked at an odd angle as if she were listening for something—most likely the ringing of the Call Me a Taxi phone—and beamed at Loren's pleasure in the meal.

"I used to be a pretty fair cook," he said. "As I got older I stopped bothering. But on my best day I never made muffins as good as these."

"Secret to making blueberry muffins is don't spare the blueberries." She poured herself coffee from the insulated carafe on the table. "A man your age, you ought to have a good woman cooking for you. This Heather gal, can she cook?"

"I have no idea," Loren said carelessly. The next moment, seeing Jessie splutter over her coffee, he realized he'd almost given away an aspect of the story he hadn't intended to share. "It's, well, sort of complicated."

"You engaged to marry her and you don't know if she can cook?"

"Welcome to the Nineties." Loren tried to cover the lameness of his answer by stuffing a large bite of hot muffin in his mouth. The next moment his throat was on fire and he downed half a huge tumbler of juice in one gulp.

"I guess," she said in a what's-this-world-coming-to tone. "You heading downtown when you finish?"

"When Jeff gets back," Loren said. "I'm more likely to run into the media if I use my own car. While I'm waiting for him do you mind if I use your phone?"

His first call was to Lewis, whose speech was punctuated by so many yawns it was obvious he hadn't slept much. "Pop's doing much better this morning and the station's sending the video over. It's only six minutes long, they didn't keep any outtakes. When will you come by?"

"Probably around eleven-thirty," Loren said. "I have a stop to make on the way."

Then he made two more calls.

The office of Bruce Unger was on the sixth and highest

story of a brick building across the street from the ancient courthouse. To Loren the top criminal defense lawyer in Dennison County looked more like a high school science teacher: frail build, birdlike gestures, spectacles, thin hair halfway between sand brown and mouse gray combed across the top of his head in a feeble attempt to hide the baldness. He sat in an executive swivel chair behind a mahogany desk polished to high gloss with his long-fingered hands folded on the inlaid leather blotter and tried to pretend he wasn't excited. "Well, naturally I'm interested, Professor. The only reason I gave you an appointment on half an hour's notice was the prospect of my representing Ms. Dennison that you held out. I am assuming of course that she wants me as her attorney and can, ah, pay my customary charges."

"I'll be seeing her at the jail later today," Loren said from the cushioned depths of the client's chair. "I can't make her ask for you but as long as you're willing I'll recommend you."

"I understand why you wouldn't want to handle the defense yourself." Unger sank his arrowhead chin in the cleft he made between his joined third and fourth fingers. "You're not admitted in Wisconsin, you don't specialize in criminal law and you're, well, too close to the case."

"Exactly," Loren agreed. "She needs someone who knows how to tweak the system here and I'm told you're the best at that."

"Of course I never prejudge," Unger said, "but from all I've read and seen on television there would seem to be a very strong case against your fiancee. Naturally, if I take her case I will act as a lawyer does and must act, as servant of what Holmes called the bad man. If he hadn't been so chivalrous he would have added the bad woman, haha. In other words I don't give a rat's ass if she killed the old bitch."

Loren kept his face bland and his disgust buried. "That's

precisely the kind of lawyer she needs."

"Do I understand you are telling me you know she is guilty?"

"I'm telling you I know she is innocent," Loren said. "While you're representing her I'm going to be doing something I'm better at than practicing law."

"And that is?"

"Finding who framed her. And not only her but someone else you're representing. Just in case you give a rat's ass about Leo McGuire, he didn't kill Phil Clift."

"Two innocent clients in one week," Unger murmured, smacking his lips together soundlessly. "How different."

Jaywalking across Main Street to the courthouse, Loren noticed two satellite vans with TV network logos threading their way through traffic and a third in a parking slot reserved for official personnel in front of the courthouse. At the next corner a TV journalist with a minicam operator behind him was stopping passersby, soliciting their comments on yesterday's brutal murder. There had been no photograph of Loren in the morning paper he had glanced through in the Wrights' living room while waiting for Jeff to return from the filling station and Jessie had said she hadn't seen any pictures of him on the TV news but he knew it wouldn't be long before the media invaders would know him by sight. Once across the street he slipped off his glasses, lowered his head and felt his way up the stone steps to the courthouse door. Once past the metal detector inside the doorway and with glasses in place again on his nose he strode to the elevator.

In Lewis' office the lights were out and the window shades drawn and the prosecutor was straddling one of the hard chairs on which he and Loren had eaten lunch two days ago. He was holding down a button on the remote unit in his hand, watching the portable video player on the upper shelf of a wheeled cart in the center of the room. Images rewound on the screen too quick for Loren to decipher. "Grab a seat," Lewis invited gruffly. "I've watched this twice already and I can't see anything out of whack." He touched the Stop and Play buttons on the remote as Loren drew up a chair. The six-minute segment began to unfold.

It opened in the studio where a TV reporter with lustrous red tresses and the general appearance of an airhead offered bromides about how physical fitness could enhance the quality of life for seniors. "One of our best known seniors is so fit she puts women half her age to shame. Civic leader and patron of the arts Lydia Dennison graciously invited I and the KDTV videocam crew into her magnificent home so that she could share her fitness secrets with our viewers." Loren made himself ignore the young woman's grammar lapse and kept focused on the images.

The scene shifted to the basement and the camera tilted upward as Lydia descended the stairs in gray sweats. She paused at the shelves in the little anteroom to select a classical audiocassette. The camera panned over the exercise room, tracked Lydia as she crossed to the wall, plugged in the tread-mill, removed the chosen cassette from its transparent plastic box, set down the box on a nondescript wooden bench against the wall, inserted the cassette into the battery-operated player attached to the exercise machine's handrail, adjusted the earphones on her head, then bent over and pressed the switch that activated the treadmill. The director of the segment spared viewers the moving belt's horrendous clanking sound, substituting Lydia herself describing in voice-over how she would gradually raise the rate of speed to 4.5 miles per hour, then after fifteen minutes or so would gradually lower the rate to 3.0 for the cool-down phase. The camera showed her shutting off the treadmill, draping her earphones over the handrail, walking towards the corner of the room that held the stall shower. Then it cut away. "After a refreshing shower," said the airhead, "Mrs. Dennison usually goes out to swim laps." Cut to an outdoor shot of Lydia diving gracefully into the pool in a black one-piece bathing suit she certainly hadn't worn when a video crew wasn't taping her swim. More voice-over narration about the joys and health benefits of aquatic exercise, then a shot of Lydia clambering out of the pool, re-entering the house through the basement door. A brief sequence in which, still wearing her bathing suit for the camera, she turned on the whirlpool, stepped down into the bubbly steaming water and soaked. Then back to the studio for some final bromides from Miss Airhead.

"Play it again," Loren said, leaning forward, attention concentrated on the screen so intensely that if a fire had broken out in the office he wouldn't have noticed. The segment unrolled again.

"There!" he cried. "Stop it right there!" Lewis touched the Freeze Frame button. "Rewind and replay the last fifteen or twenty seconds." The prosecutor touched other buttons. "See it? See it?"

"See what?" Lewis demanded.

"The little plastic box the audiocassette came from. Watch her set it down on that old garden bench."

"Well, she has to put it somewhere and she's neat so she doesn't toss it on the floor."

"Keep watching," Loren told him.

Lydia finishing her treadmill routine. Removing her earphones, draping them over the handrail, moving towards the shower. "Freeze it," Loren said. "Now, tell me what you did *not* see her do."

Lewis stared at him without comprehension.

"She did not take the audiocassette out of the player," Loren said. "She did not put the cassette back in its box. She did not return the box to its place on the shelves in the anteroom."

"Well, of course she didn't," Lewis snorted. "She's dripping with sweat after forty-five minutes on that treadmill."

"When she's alone, when the camera's not there, what's she going to do next?"

"Get naked in a hurry and jump in that shower," Lewis answered.

"And after the shower?"

"Into the pool."

"When does she return the cassette to its box and the box to the shelves?"

"I don't know. Later, after she finishes her laps. Maybe after she gets out of the whirlpool. That's the way I'd do it, wouldn't you . . ." Then he saw where Loren's train of thought was going. "Oh my God," he whispered.

"Yesterday the murderer interrupted her routine," Loren pointed out. "He attacked her as she was getting out of the pool. So when you and Stacy and the police came out, why wasn't the cassette she listened to on the treadmill still in the player? Why wasn't the box it came from still on the garden bench? You didn't see them there, did you?"

Lewis shook his head groggily like a punch-drunk prizefighter.

"So what does that tell us?" Loren went on. "That the murderer, after he killed Lydia, boxed the cassette himself and either returned it to the shelves or took it with him."

"That's insane," Lewis growled.

"No, it only seems insane because we don't know yet why he took the trouble to do it. The key to why he did it is

179

figuring what music Lydia was listening to before he killed her. There are two ways we might be able to do that. If he took the tape with him and she kept a catalogue of her cassettes, we should be able to tell which one is missing. If he returned it to the shelves he probably wiped his fingerprints off the box first, so if we have every cassette box on the shelves checked for prints and one turns out to be clean, that's the tape we want."

Lewis kicked back his chair and began to pace the office savagely. "Prosecutors don't keep fingerprint equipment around. I'd better call Stacy about this."

"Sit down," Loren said. "We don't need Stacy yet. I called the FBI office in Madison this morning and told the agent in charge we may be dealing with a serial killer down here. They're sending a team. Meanwhile you and I have to talk about something else I saw on that video."

Lewis stalked to his desk and dropped into the battered oak swivel chair behind it.

"Remember what we know about the security system in Lydia's house," Loren continued. "If the code hasn't been punched in within thirty seconds before or after a door opens, an alarm goes off loud enough to wake the dead." Lewis said nothing. "Now you can't see this on the videotape because there was a cut from the exercise room to the pool yard, but just before Lydia goes out to the pool through that basement door she has to punch in the code. Yes?"

"With you so far," Lewis said.

"And when she goes from the pool back into the basement through that door, she has to punch in the code again within thirty seconds of re-entering the house?"

"Yeah," Lewis agreed.

"Now," Loren said, "think back to your reconstruction of the murder. The killer attacks Lydia as she's climbing out of the pool. Clubs her several times. Blood is streaming down her face. She runs in blind panic back into the basement through that unlocked door with the murderer on her heels. Is she going to stop to punch in the code? Of course not! The only thing that may save her life is if the alarm goes off and Fraser runs over! But we know the alarm did not go off because Fraser would have heard it in his apartment and come over on the run if it had. Therefore the murderer must have stopped for a moment in his pursuit of Lydia to punch in the code. Which is changed every two weeks!"

"So you're claiming the murderer must have known three things," Lewis cut in, "namely Lydia's new codicil, her exercise routine—*and* the alarm code. Excuse me for screwing up your Charlie Chan act, Professor, but haven't you just dug your own grave? I mean, who besides Lydia would have known the current code? Fraser, the housekeeper—and Heather."

"We're going to have to learn more about Fraser and the housekeeper. But why would either of them have replaced or taken away the audiocassette? And what motive for killing Lydia would they have? Somebody else *must* have known the code. Speaking of motive," Loren went on, snapping open his attaché case and handing his copy of Almon Dennison's trust instrument over the desk, "look at this. Just the page I dog-eared."

Lewis stifled a yawn and flipped through the pages.

"I suggested to you last night," Loren said, "that the murderer must have intended not only to kill Lydia but to frame Heather for it. Why frame Heather? So that after she was convicted a suit could be brought to set aside the codicil in her favor. Now, who would have standing to bring such a suit? Well, there are two possibilities. One is a suit by the Cultural Foundation to reinstate Lydia's previous exercise of her power of appointment, which would divert fifty percent of the trust corpus into the Foundation's treasury. Who'd benefit from such a suit? Just about everyone who makes their living from the arts in this town. That gives us one circle of suspects. But there's another possibility. Someone might sue to set aside Lydia's final exercise of her power *without* reinstating her previous exercise of it, so that the fifty percent of corpus that she had power of appointment over would be disposed of as if she'd never exercised her power at all. Now, who would have standing to bring such a suit? Before I went to sleep last night I hunted through the trust instrument and found what it provided in case Lydia should die without having exercised her power. It's on the page I dog-eared."

Lewis' lips moved slightly as he scanned the paragraphs Loren had indicated. "Do I read this gobbledygook right? If she died without exercising her power, the half of the trust corpus that generated her income would be sort of blended into the rest of the corpus so every other living beneficiary's share shoots way up."

"Precisely," Loren said. "In other words, any other living beneficiary who knows the three things you mentioned has a huge financial incentive to kill Lydia and frame Heather. And those are the exact same people who had motive to kill off every beneficiary who died before Lydia! Unless you want to believe yesterday's murder has no connection with the earlier deaths among Almon Dennison's relatives, it seems pretty clear that Lydia was killed by our friend Alec."

"Jesus," Lewis muttered. Then he lifted his head and stared bleary-eyed at Loren. "You forgot the cane," he said then. "Lydia was clubbed to death with Heather's cane. So if the murderer wasn't Heather, how the hell could he have known Heather's cane was lying there in the basement?"

"That's an excellent question," Loren agreed. "I thought

of it too. Maybe the answer's in the Yellow Pages." He stood up, crossed the office as if he owned it and took the directory from the scarred bookcase behind Lewis' desk. "Mattresses," he said under his breath. "Meat Markets. Medical Business Administration. Ah, here we are. Looks like the only place I need to visit is Dennison Medical Equipment and Supplies. 65 Grove Street."

"That's a couple blocks from here, over on Historical Square," Lewis told him.

"Don't go to lunch for a while, okay?" Loren asked. "I'll be back soon."

"If I get lunch at all it'll be right here, there's a ton of phone calls I haven't returned."

Loren would have bet anything that one of those calls was from Domjan in New York, and that before the prosecutor had finished wolfing down his deli sandwich he would know he had a nun in jail.

A scatter of tourists gave him cover from prowling media people as he walked the two city blocks from the courthouse to the premises of Dennison Medical Equipment and Supplies, which turned out to be on the same side of the Historical Square that housed a music store, two restaurants, a Classical Coffee Company, a bookshop and an ice cream parlor. He stepped through the doorway and entered a world of white-painted steel shelving under fluorescents. Crutches, wheelchairs, walkers, support stockings, diabetic kits, infant nursing kits, a section marked BOUTIQUE that was partitioned off so women customers could be fitted in privacy for breast prostheses. Behind a formica counter at the far end of the store stood a young man with straw-colored hair and buck teeth. "How can I be of service to you today?" he inquired brightly.

"I'd like to see your canes," Loren said. What had struck him in Lewis' office was that the murderer would not have needed to know Heather had left her cane in Lydia's exercise room; he might have brought a similar one of his own, used it to kill Lydia, and taken away Heather's so as to make it appear her cane had been the murder weapon. Loren had come here to find out if anyone else had recently purchased a cane like Heather's but on the way over he had realized she would need a new one. Might as well buy it for her, he had decided, and bring it to her when he visited the jail.

"You seem to be walking perfectly fine, sir, as far as I can see," the clerk said.

"It's not for me." Loren saw no reason to add that it was for a woman charged with a brutal murder.

"This way then." The youth scooted out from behind the counter and led the way to an alcove where an assortment of canes was displayed on a revolving rack. "This is our stock, sir."

There were wood canes and aluminum canes and lucite canes, some with handles in the shape of a duck or fish head, some with heads that resembled a flowing distorted T. None of the wooden canes had the traditional curved handle like the one Heather had used. Loren asked where those canes were kept.

"Wooden with a curved handle?" the clerk echoed with a dumbfounded look in his violet eyes. "We don't see those very often. Aluminum canes are much better." He snatched one from the rack and brandished it. "They give more support and—see here?—the length's adjustable."

The consternation seemed to migrate from the youth's face to Loren's. "You are the only medical supply house in Dennison?"

"Yes, sir. Been here twenty-seven years."

"Well then, you must have sold at least one wooden cane with a curved handle last week. Don't you remember the young woman who was hit on the kneecap out at Nature's Ovens?"

"I remember the story in the papers, sure. The babe's in jail now, she killed an old broad yesterday." He ran a hand through his unruly mop of hair and stood taller as if he expected his picture to be taken. "I bet you're one of those TV guys been pouring into town since the murder, right? Can you put me on TV?"

Loren pretended to consider the request. "There might be a spot for you," he said cautiously. "But I'm confused. Are you telling me this shop didn't sell the cane Heather Dennison was using since she was attacked?"

"You mean the cane she beat the old broad to death with? Of course we didn't sell it! The other clerk's sick, I've been on duty here every day we've been open for the past ten days. No one else but me could have sold her a cane and if I had they would have put me on TV last night or this morning."

"Shit," Loren said, and swung around and made his way up the aisles and out of the shop, asking himself over and over: *Then where the hell did the cane come from?*

The moment he stepped out into the street, he found the answer staring him in the face.

He double-timed back to the courthouse, cursed the delay at the metal detector, raced to the elevator bank, tore through the district attorney's outer office and into the sanctum where Lewis was sitting at his desk with the phone to his ear. "Good . . . Thanks for the information, sir. Yes, I'll keep you informed . . . See you soon." He hung up the phone, yawned, turned to Loren. "You won't be happy to learn your hunch was right," he said.

"What hunch?" Loren asked, his thoughts elsewhere.

"The one you threw out at the hospital last night, about the inner circle in this town finding out about Lydia's new codicil and her plan to support Heather's battered women's shelter. She told Ward Dennison at the bank, he told Clay Brean and Dan Feinberg and yesterday they had a sort of emergency meeting about the effect on the local economy if Lydia started throwing her money at the shelter instead of the Cultural Foundation."

"Why should that make me unhappy?"

"Because the meeting ran till almost six P.M.," Lewis answered. "Or to put it another way, they all alibi each other for the time Lydia was killed. Not that they're under any suspicion but you've been harping on the idea that some beneficiary's been killing a bunch of others and this alibi rules out a couple of your prime suspects at least on Lydia's murder."

"How do we know all three of them aren't in a conspiracy together?" Loren demanded.

"Because their meeting was at Mayor Wolfe's office," Lewis explained with the sigh of a long-suffering father whose child is addicted to silly questions, "and both he and the deputy mayor were there too. That was Ralph Wolfe I was on the phone with a minute ago."

"Oh," Loren said.

"Now suppose you tell me why you barged in here so ex-cited," the prosecutor suggested.

It actually took Loren several seconds before he remembered. "The cane," he said then. "Heather's cane. It didn't come from the only medical supply house in town. *It came from Almon Dennison.* God, I've been dense! My first hour in town I sat through that Chamber of Commerce video with the old footage of him walking with a cane, and the statue of him in the center of the Historical Square shows him with a cane too!"

"Of course it came from the old man. Anyone who grew up here when he was alive could have told you that. He always carried one wherever he walked. He didn't need it, just used it like, you know, like Charlie Chaplin. A visual gimmick."

"If only someone had mentioned it! You didn't, Lydia didn't, Heather didn't . . ."

"There was no secret about it. After Heather was whacked Lydia gave her one of Almon's canes to use till she could walk without support. The old man had a collection of them."

"How many were in the collection?" Loren demanded.

"How the hell would I know?" Then Lewis buried his chin in his palm and his eyes went vacant as if he were wandering in the mists of memory. "Two or three times a year when I was a kid," he said softly, "Almon's vice-presidents and their families would be invited to the house for a Sunday afternoon picnic. I remember one of those parties, I was maybe ten or eleven and Almon and Lydia invited Pop and me into the master bedroom suite and Almon took this beautiful polished teak box out of his closet and opened it for us. It was, I don't know, maybe four feet tall, and there were receptacles in it for each of his canes. I can't remember how many canes were in the box. Six, eight. Damn but he was proud of them."

"Is that box still at the house now?"

"Must be. Lydia took over the master suite after Almon died and I know she kept the canes, to remember him by I guess. The box is probably still in the same closet."

"If we went out there now and counted the canes in that box, how many empty receptacles do you think we'd find?"

Lewis thought for a few seconds. "One," he said then. "And the cane that belongs there is in the PD evidence locker."

"Suppose we found two vacant slots?" Loren asked.

ELEVEN

The dusty Honda Civic slid out of downtown Dennison, through the near suburbs, out into the gentle hills where cows sprawled in pastures under clouds like cotton candy. Lewis drove in a silence Loren dared not break. They turned onto a long straight road from which at the edge of vision the Dennison mansion seemed the size of a dollhouse, with what looked like a dot circling above its roof. "Media chopper," Lewis grunted. The Honda passed beneath the stone archway. Two uniforms ran forward as Lewis parked, then drew back deferentially as they recognized the man stepping out from the driver's seat as the district attorney. "No one else around?" Lewis asked.

The older cop gestured towards the whirling blades overhead. "Only those guys, whoever they are."

"This is an official visit and this gentleman is with me," Lewis said. "We're not going near the crime scene, just upstairs. We won't be long. Any objections?"

The cop dug a ring of keys from his trousers pocket. "Captain Stacy gave me the alarm code, sir. I'll punch it in for you and then just wait at the foot of the stairs till you're through."

Lewis led the way up the marble staircase, down the long corridor, past the closed door to what had been Heather's room. "God, this brings back memories." With the hesitancy of a small boy in a strange and lavish world he opened the door to the master suite.

It was cool, bright, high-ceilinged, larger than many studio apartments, and so neat Loren could hardly believe it had been used regularly for years. The canopied bed with a quilt over its spread could have held four people. Wood surfaces glowed with polish, brushes and combs and crystal bottles stood in perfect order on a vanity top. One open door revealed a luxurious bathroom, another connected with a dressing room which in turn connected with the room Heather had been using. As Lewis opened the third door a light came on and displayed a long deep closet fitted with teak cabinets for shoes. Loren saw cocktail gowns, street dresses, evening wear, silk blouses, dark slacks, a few pairs of jeans, everything on wooden or padded satin hangers, no item jammed too close to any other. He caught the faint lilac scent of Lydia's perfume. Lewis went down on one knee, reached underneath the dresses, tugged out a waist-high mahogany box from the rear of the closet, set it upright in the doorway and lifted its lid.

The hand-carved box held six gleaming canes and empty slots for two more.

"As I thought," Loren said softly. "These six canes look all but identical. The missing two almost certainly look the same. Our Alec brought one of those with him for his weapon. After he killed Lydia he found the other one, the cane Heather had left in the exercise room, and took it away with him."

"Or else Heather's the murderer and Lydia gave the missing cane to somebody years ago as a keepsake," Lewis suggested, and carefully replaced the cabinet behind Lydia's gowns in the closet. "Let's get out of here, I'm getting a creepy feeling."

Before they were out of the master suite Loren heard a hollow cheeping sound that seemed to be coming from the prosecutor's innards as if he were carrying a baby chick in his pocket. Lewis reached inside his jacket and withdrew a cell phone. "Yeah . . . He's right here." He turned to Loren and offered him the handset. "For you," he said.

Loren took the phone with puzzlement on his face and heard in his ear the unmistakable voice of Jeff Wright. "Where are you, man?" the driver asked.

"With Mr. Lewis at the Dennison house. We were just about to leave . . ."

"Don't you go nowhere," Wright said. "Something's come up."

"What?" Loren demanded.

"I was home eating lunch with Jessie a while ago when I got a call you need to know about. You said you'd be seeing the DA this morning so I called there and his secretary said the both of you had gone out but if you was still together she could reach you on his cell phone . . . Look, you just stay at the house, I'm on my way, I gotta tell you about this call."

"What was so special about it?"

"Well, for one thing," Wright said, "it was in German."

The cop secured the house behind them and left them pacing the parking area in the front yard. Loren strode the edge of the grass at close to a jog and fought the feeling that Heather would be better served if there were a way of keeping from Lewis whatever Wright had learned. Ten minutes later he heard brakes squealing and the burgundy station wagon careened into the drive. Wright leapt out of the cab as Loren and Lewis trotted towards him. Hastily and hoping he wasn't revealing too much, Loren performed the introductions. "Lydia arranged for Mr. Wright to be my driver while my car was being fixed," he explained, then turned to Jeff and, knowing the ploy's chance of success was nil, said in a pathetic imitation of an off-the-cuff thought: "If you want to take me back to town I'm sure Mr. Lewis wouldn't mind."

"Maybe you both better hear about this," Wright said, and Loren clamped his teeth together. "When you do I don't think you'll want to go back to town right away. It's about Miss Lydia's murder."

At the end of the few minutes it took Wright to recount the story, Loren felt like a man reborn into a better world. The sky was bluer, the air purer, birds in the distant trees sang a sweeter song. "By God," Lewis muttered. "I was so sure . . . We may have locked up an innocent person."

"Let's find out," Loren said.

It was after two and the Alpendenn dining room was empty except for the slack-faced busboys cleaning the place and the four men hunched at a corner table with coffee turning cold in their cups. Anders Nordsten told his story again, in German that for the most part Loren was able to follow, interspersed with an occasional few words of what the tall athletic Dane took to be English. "He tried to call the police first," Loren explained to the prosecutor, "but no one on the switchboard spoke German. He had Mr. Wright's business card and knew he was fluent in German because the three of us happened to have lunch out here yesterday."

"I got that part," Lewis said. "I know a little of the language myself. Not as good as you guys."

"He's a champion long-distance runner in Denmark," Loren went on, determined to insure that Lewis understood the entire story, "and plans to enter the New York Marathon in the fall. Most weekday afternoons when he's finished his research out here he changes into gym clothes and does a 26-mile practice run."

"I know for a fact that's the truth," Wright interjected.

"The professor and I were out on the back roads in my cab just the other day and crossed his path."

"His run yesterday happened to take him past where the private drive to the Dennison house opens off that county road. He can't swear to the exact time but puts it between five-thirty and six."

"*Ja ja,*" Nordsten said. "*Sicherlich zwischen halb sechs und sechs.*"

"That," Loren continued, "was when he noticed a car parked in a grove of trees, about a quarter mile from the entrance to the private drive."

"I didn't quite get what kind of car," Lewis admitted.

"Neither did he," Wright said.

"The car wasn't meant to be seen," Loren added. "In any event Mr. Nordsten isn't all that familiar with American cars and he was running at top speed so he only saw it for a few seconds. He says it was bigger than a Volkswagen but smaller than a limousine and either dark gray or blue. Maybe black."

"Big help," Lewis grunted.

"He also saw a piece of the license plate," Loren said.

The prosecutor sat straighter in his chair. "By damn, that part went over my head. Does he remember what numbers he saw?"

"There weren't any numbers," Loren said.

"All plates in this state have numbers," Lewis insisted. "Three letters, a dash, three numbers."

"Not vanity plates," Loren corrected him. "Mr. Nordsten says the plate he saw consisted entirely of letters. The only ones he can remember are the first two."

"Herr Nordsten," Lewis began, and cleared his throat. "Err—*was waren die Letters was Sie sah?*"

Loren deduced from the confused look on the Dane's face that the prosecutor's version of the language of Goethe was

Greek to him and, in more conventional syntax, asked Nordsten to tell them what letters he remembered seeing. The answer came back without hesitation and in something like English.

"Kay Ohh," Nordsten said slowly.

"Don't you make the connection?" Loren demanded. "Don't you see the picture?"

They were in the station wagon again, gentle green slopes rolling by through the side windows, blissful blue sky at the horizon, Lewis' Honda and a bewildered Nordsten left behind at the cheese factory. Loren sat on the edge of the cab's backseat, his body turned towards the prosecutor's at a sharp angle, while Jeff Wright tried to keep his eyes on the lightly traveled county road and his attention on the conversation behind him.

"The car Lydia's killer used has a license plate that begins with KO and contains no numbers, just more letters. Therefore it must have been a vanity plate. Assuming it's one of the plates Lydia financed to promote classical music, it must have six letters, no more and no less."

"How the hell could you possibly know that?" Lewis growled.

"Cause I told him so Sunday, the first time I drove him," Wright volunteered. "Didn't you notice the plate on this cab, Mr. Lewis? I had to leave the T out of SATCHMO to get six letters."

"Now," Loren went on, "try to put yourself in the exercise room immediately after Lydia's murder. The killer knows he has to get out of there in a hurry but he's experienced enough at killing to take a quick look around and make sure nothing is there that will point to him. What does he see?"

There was silence in the moving cage. Wright stuck his

head out the driver's side window and, when he was sure the road was clear, sped up and swerved into the opposite lane to pass a crawling farm truck.

"He sees the box that held the cassette Lydia was listening to on her last walk," Loren said. "And what does the box show him? The same name that's on his own license plate! It spooks him. So he either puts the cassette and its box back on the shelves or he takes it with him and destroys it later. Can you give me any other explanation that fits what we know?"

"Okay," Lewis agreed. "You've cleared up one thing the guy did. First thing I do when we're back in town, I call Madison, send for the doctor the PD uses to put crime victims and witnesses under hypnosis when we need them to remember more than they consciously recall. Maybe the rest of the letters on that license plate are buried in Nordsten's subconscious."

"There may be a much faster way," Loren said. "That's why we're not going back to town yet."

The cab turned at a cloverleaf intersection and merged into the heavier traffic of a four-lane state highway. Amid the sedans and semis and RVs a road sign slid by: DENNISON COMMUNITY COLLEGE NEXT EXIT. From the top of the next rise Loren saw the cluster of long low buildings in the distance.

"Tell me one person connected with classical music whose name has or can be reduced to six letters and begins with KO," Loren challenged.

"Ain't my field of expertise," Wright replied. Lewis screwed his features into a mask of intense concentration like a contestant on a TV game show.

"I can think of just one," Loren told them. "Our next stop is to find out if there are more."

★ ★ ★ ★ ★

Wright let them out in front of the college library and drove on in search of a parking slot. Loren and Lewis made their way through a knot of students sunning themselves on the broad low steps. Inside the double doors the security guard who they showed their ID to pointed them towards the reference department across the main room. Students stood over each of the dozen computer terminals that served as the library's catalogue. Loren stopped at the octagonal information kiosk, asked a question, copied down figures on a slip of paper, then with Lewis a few paces behind him trotted to a long row of shelves full of outsize volumes: encyclopedias, concordances, directories, gazetteers, bibliographies, reference works on everything from American Jewish authors to science fiction films to precisely what he was hunting for. "We're here," he announced, careful to keep his voice low, and lifted his hand to indicate the twenty volumes of the New Grove Dictionary of Music and Musicians. He plucked from its mates Volume 10, Kern to Lindelheim, held it firmly under his arm as if afraid it might be snatched from him and stalked out of the reference area to the corner of the main room where stood a bank of photocopy machines. One had an OUT OF ORDER placard on it, two were in use. The fourth seemed to be functioning and free. "Stand here," Loren ordered the prosecutor. "Don't move." He dug into his wallet, extracted five singles, passed each in turn through the dollar bill changer at the end of the row of photocopiers, and returned with fifty dimes to where Lewis was standing.

When they left the library and wandered through the parking lot in search of Wright's cab, Loren had no dimes left and fifty double sheets of photocopy paper in his breast pocket. He heard a horn honk and the next minute the burgundy wagon slid to a stop beside them. They clambered into

195

the back seat. "Downtown," Loren said absently, and as the cab swerved out of the lot and off campus he pulled the papers from his pocket and ran his eyes down them in a frenzy of absorption that allowed no room for Lewis or Wright or anything else in the world. Five miles down the road he came out of his trance, raised his eyes to Lewis and handed him the papers.

"I was right," he said. "An amazing number of composers have names that begin with KO but there's only one whose name has six letters and who's well enough known to have been a likely candidate for a vanity plate. Ever hear of Zoltán Kodály?" Guessing that Lewis hadn't, he spelled out the last name.

The prosecutor tossed sheets of photocopy paper on the cab floor until he found the relevant pages. "Yeah, here he is . . . Hungarian. Lived from 1882 to 1967. Best known for the orchestral suite from—I can't read this small print while we're moving, is it Hairy Jason?"

"*Háry János,*" Loren corrected him.

"Never heard of it."

"Me neither," Wright echoed. The cab turned off the state highway and the elegant homes of Dennison's outer suburbs came into view. "By the way, you mind telling me where I'm supposed to be taking you gentlemen next?"

"That depends entirely on you," Loren answered. "Do you remember telling me how you stopped Lydia on the street one day and asked if you could have a plate with a black musician's name on it and she said of course you could?"

"Remember it like it was yesterday," Wright said. "Maybe cause it was only two days before yesterday I told you."

"After she agreed, what did you do then?"

"I got my SACHMO plate," Wright said.

"No, no, I mean didn't you have to go somewhere to—

well, sign up for that particular plate?"

"Course I did."

"Where did you have to go? What I'm trying to find out is who administered this vanity plate project for Lydia, who kept track of what plates everyone wanted?"

"Oh, yeah, I see where you're headed now. I went to the Cultural Foundation. Dennison Hall, fourth floor. Man in charge was named Weingold, Feingold, Weinstein, Feinstein . . ."

"Feinberg?" Loren suggested.

"That's it, Feinberg. Actually his secretary was the one took down the information from me."

"Then we see her next," Loren said.

Wright dropped them at the front entrance of Dennison Hall. As they mounted the ornate marble steps they saw him turn into the alley that led to the parking lot behind the building. They strode through the vast atrium with its domed ceiling six stories above the ground level, took an elevator to the fourth floor and entered the Cultural Foundation's outer office where Mary Dougherty, with her turquoise-framed glasses and flame-orange hair, sat behind her desk tapping away at her computer keyboard. "May I help . . ." she began, then looked up from her screen. "Oh, I remember you from the other day," she said to Loren. "I'm sorry, Dan's not in right now."

"It's you we need to see," he told her. "Mr. Lewis here is the district attorney."

A look of panic spread over the woman's freckled face as if she expected to be arrested the next moment.

"Were you working here back when Lydia Dennison offered to pay for vanity license plates that had a classical music connection?" Lewis asked her.

"Why, yes! I've been Dan's secretary for five years now."

"And everyone who wanted in on that offer had to see you?"

"That's right. I must have had a hundred people come through here, Dan had me keep the records."

"How did you keep them?" Loren asked.

She stared at him as if he had asked an incredibly dense question, like whether she spoke English. "On computer disk," she said. "Naturally."

"You kept a disk that would tell you who asked for what name on their vanity plates?"

"How else would I remember, sir?" she inquired sweetly.

"Do you still have it?" *Please, please let her have the disk,* he said silently.

The question made her face go strawberry red. "Gosh, that was awhile back . . . If it's not on disk maybe it's still on my hard drive . . ." She opened a drawer, pulled out a container designed to hold a dozen disks, flipped through their labels, extracted another container from the same drawer. "I don't recall erasing it . . . Here, here it is, license plates." She thrust the disk into the hard card slot on her unit, touched keys, stared at the bright blue screen until the proper file appeared. "What do you want to know?"

Loren heard his heart pound. "Who applied for the KODALY plate?" Seeing her face go blank at the Hungarian pronunciation ko-dye, he spelled the name out for her.

The secretary touched more keys, then stared at the screen as if hypnotized. "Nobody," she said.

The reply struck Loren like a blow to the solar plexus. "Nobody?" he repeated stupidly. "Are you telling me there is no license plate in this county with the letters KODALY?"

"Well, if there is it didn't come through this office and Mrs. Dennison didn't pay for it," she insisted.

"Shit," Loren said. Without remembering to thank her he stalked out of the office with Lewis in his wake.

They took the stairs down to the atrium and Lewis led them through narrow corridors to a rear exit. "Might as well take a short cut to the lot," he said. They threaded their way through a knot of nicotine addicts taking a smoke break on the outside stoop and descended four steps to the paved lot where three rows of cars basked in the afternoon sun. "I don't see Wright's cab, maybe he couldn't find a slot. Come on, let's go around to the street. Some brilliant theory," he remarked acidly as they walked along one of the twin lanes to the alley entrance. "The murderer had to have KODALY on his plate. No one has KODALY on his plate. I suppose that means no one's the murderer!"

"There's another answer," Loren muttered disconsolately. "There has to be."

"Find it for me, genius," Lewis said.

It was less than ten seconds after the challenge that Loren froze in his tracks as if he had suffered a stroke. His heart stopped. His mind stopped. "I don't believe . . . It can't . . ."

"Are you all right, man?"

"Look!" Loren cried out. "Look!" He seized the prosecutor's beefy shoulders, spun him around in the direction of a tan Lincoln Continental sandwiched in the middle row between a Hyundai and an Isuzu. "The plate! The plate!"

Lewis stared uncomprehending at the six letters on the Lincoln's plate. "That's not . . ." he began.

"The hell it's not!" Loren raced back towards the door that opened on the parking lot, pulled frantically at the knob, and found that, while perfectly good for letting anyone out of the building, it would not let anyone in unless they had a key. He wheeled around, ran the length of the lot, through the alley, around to the front door and into the atrium again. The elevator indicator showed that the cage was on the way up with other passengers. "Stairs," Loren said, and took them two at a time to the fourth floor. By the time he flung open the door to the Cultural Foundation's outer office he could feel a vague throbbing in his left arm. Mary Dougherty half rose from her desk and stared at them as if they had invaded her workspace with AK-47s.

"In the lot," Loren said, trying to keep calm, willing himself not to be having an angina attack. "Lincoln Continental. Tan. Sunroof. License plate SHOSTA."

"What the fuck does a mountain in California have to do with this?" a panting Lewis demanded.

"Shut up," Loren said, and sat down in the visitor chair. His arm stopped throbbing after a minute. "Who owns that Lincoln?" he asked the secretary. "Please," he thought to say then. "This is really important."

"Why, it's Ellis Carr's," she said. "You know, he manages KDEN, his office is downstairs, third floor."

Ellis Carr. Loren remembered being introduced to him at Lydia's party but had no recollection of what he looked like. "Where's the other half of the plate?" he demanded.

"Sir," Mary told him frigidly, "I don't have the slightest idea what you're referring to."

"KOVICH!" he all but shouted. "Kovich!"

The secretary tapped keys, stared at her screen. "You could have asked me before, you know," she said. "It's on my list right below KODALY but you never . . ."

"I know. I know. I'm sorry. Please forgive me," Loren said. "Who got the KOVICH license plate?"

"I don't have to look at the screen, I can see the car right through this window, the dark blue Caddy in the middle of the rear row."

He wanted to scream. The truth was blazing like a fire in front of all three of them but he was the only one who could see it because Lewis and the secretary had never heard of Dmitri Shostakovich. God, God, it was all so obvious now! Every vanity plate in Lydia's package had to have six letters but why couldn't a twelve-letter name be spread over two plates? SHOSTA on one, KOVICH on the other. And Ellis Carr was married to . . .

"The cellist," Loren said, and groped for her name from Sunday evening at Lydia's house. Very slender, floor-length black dress, eyes that had kept blinking at him from behind gold-framed spectacles. What was her name? "Wentz. Manya Wentz. She owns the Cadillac? She got the KOVICH plate?"

"That's what it says here," Mary Dougherty said, and tapped an orange fingernail at the computer screen. Loren came over behind her desk to look at the screen for himself and she pushed her secretarial chair back towards the wall and window to make room for him. "There she goes now," she said.

"What? Who?"

"Manya Wentz," Mary said, and nodded towards the window that looked out on the rear parking lot. "She and some man I don't know are crossing the lot towards her car."

Loren's heart thundered again. He pushed her aside, stared through the window to the lot with its aisles and the triple row of cars. He made out two figures but they were too far below and his eyes were too weak to identify either. "Are you sure that's her?" he demanded.

"I see her coming and going several days a week," Mary insisted. "That's her. Look at the way that guy's got her by the elbow. I don't think she wants to go with him."

Loren didn't stop to look. "Come on!" he shouted at Lewis. They rushed out of the office and slammed the door behind them and ran to the elevator. The indicator placed it on the ground floor. "Stairs," Loren gasped. "Fast!" He took them on the run without looking back to see if Lewis was behind him. On the atrium level he retraced their route through side corridors to the back door and flung it open and found the stoop empty of smokers and squeezed between parked cars and ran across the parallel lanes to the rear of the lot where the Cadillac was just backing out. Loren couldn't see which of the two was behind the wheel. He planted himself in the car's path and stood there like a boulder and the Cad's horn blasted and Loren didn't move and Lewis came up and stood motionless beside him. He heard a muffled shout from inside the Cad. "Run him over, you bitch, run him over!"

The burgundy station wagon turned into the lane and came slowly along the rear row as if Wright were hunting for a vacant slot. The Cad inched closer to the men's legs and Loren heard more shouting from inside the car and brakes screeched and the cab stopped dead in the middle of the lane and Jeff Wright pushed his head out the driver's side window. "What is going on here . . ."

"Get out!" Loren screamed at him. "This is Lydia's killer! Get help!"

"Don't need it! Move!" Wright gunned the engine and Loren and Lewis ran back between two cars in the middle row and the cab crashed into the right rear of the Cadillac and the impact slewed the Cad into the Buick Regal parked next to it and the passenger door flew open and a man emerged with madness in his eyes and a .357 Magnum in his hand. Without aiming he fired three shots into the Cad's interior and there was a high thin scream and he swung the weapon around and fired at the cab and its windshield shattered and he swung again and the barrel of his weapon sought Loren and Lewis who had taken cover behind cars in the middle row. People began poking their heads out the rear door of Dennison Hall and a police cruiser with siren wailing tore into the lot and screeched to a halt behind the cab and two uniforms leaped out with pistols drawn and the man with the gun vaulted over the long hood of the Cad and slithered between the fronts of the cars in the rear row and the blank concrete wall of the building beyond the lot and fired wildly at whatever moved and then crouched low and on the diagonal he raced across the rear lane and between cars and across the middle lane and between cars and up the four steps to the rear door of Dennison Hall but the people who had been poking their heads out were gone and the self-locking door was shut and the killer tugged at the latch and nothing happened and tore at it and nothing happened and the uniforms closed in and Loren and Lewis on their bellies on the pavement edged closer and the man seemed about to leap down from the four steps and then seemed to change his mind and stuck his pistol in his mouth and squeezed the trigger and there was a hollow boom and the rear door of the haven for chamber music was smeared with his blood and brains and the bones of his skull. The uniforms kept crouched low as they approached what was left of him. Loren struggled to his feet and found Lewis' arm around him. His arm throbbed. His heart roared. He leaned against the hood of the nearest car and hyper-ventilated. The uniforms were standing at the foot of the rear steps looking down at the faceless ruin. Through a haze of pain Loren saw one of them point at something wrapped around the dead man's neck. Something in a shade of red lighter than the blood that drenched it.

"Jesus God," the cop breathed. "It's Captain Stacy."

TWELVE

He was in a hospital shroud and lying on his back on a padded table in a room so cold it might have been the inside of a butcher's freezer. Masked, gowned figures formed an oval around him. One of them gave him tranquilizers and a local anesthetic and when the drugs took hold another of the gowned figures inserted a catheter into his inner thigh near the groin. Words came muffled through the facemask. "There is a slight risk that when the dye reaches your heart you'll have an adverse reaction." He felt a warm flush radiating outward from his chest. With a kind of sick fascination as if he had slipped out of his body and were watching an autopsy on himself, he focused on the video monitor three feet above his head, on the gray screen that showed him his pumping heart and the arteries feeding it blood. The images seemed to hypnotize him. He had no idea how much time had slipped by before he heard the mask-muffled voice again. "Just one artery blocked. Another angioplasty will do you. If there's a next time I think it will have to be bypass surgery."

The tranquilizers inside him defanged the words, transformed them into a subject of intellectual interest, not a kind of death sentence. "How do I keep something like this from happening again?" he asked.

"Change your life," the muffled voice told him. An image invaded his memory: Lydia sitting on a hotel couch beside him, quoting from a poem by Rilke.

Attendants wheeled him out and into a sort of storage room and then into another operating room or perhaps the same one where they had done the angiogram. Once again they inserted a catheter and he watched the monitor as the microscopic instrument coursed through his bloodstream like a toy boat on an ocean. At the point of blockage a tiny balloon in the catheter inflated and pushed the plaque back against the artery's walls so blood could flow through freely.

When they returned him to his room on the top floor of Dennison Memorial Hospital it was night. Loren slept. When he came awake the gap beneath the window shade still showed black. "I'm alive," he said to the shadowed room. He pressed the bedside button and uncountable minutes later a woman in starched white opened the door to the corridor. "What time is it?" he asked weakly.

"Ten-fifteen, honey. Anything I can do for you?"

"Is there a TV in this room?"

The nurse touched a switch and the room was bathed in a soft cone of light. "Sure is. One in every room, no extra charge." She handed him the remote unit from the bedside table.

"My glasses?" he asked.

She took them from the table drawer and gently adjusted them on his nose, then depressed a button that lifted the head of the bed. He thanked her, found and touched the Power button.

The first channel that came on the screen was a local network affiliate and the only topic on the ten o'clock news was the violent events of the day. Loren had missed the first fifteen minutes but learned from the rest of the program much that he hadn't known. The credits were unwinding on the screen bracketed to the wall when there was a soft knock on the door and the same nurse stood in the opening. "Are you up to a visitor, sir?" Loren couldn't make out the figure that stood behind her in the corridor.

"I guess so," he said, and turned the set off. Jeff Wright ambled into the dim-lit room and stood awkwardly at the foot of the bed.

"Watching the coverage, I see," he said. "Ain't much else on unless they give you satellite or cable."

"I turned it on late and things aren't connecting too well. You know I did just get out of surgery."

"That's why I dropped by," Wright said. "Make sure you were okay."

"How about yourself?"

"Not a scratch on me but my windshield's gone and there's big damage from where I plowed into that Caddy. Lucky none of those shots hit my cell phone. That's how come the paramedics got to you so quick."

"I owe you," Loren said. "But why didn't you just drive like hell out of that lot and get help the way I said?"

Wright made his way to a hard chair beside the bed and lowered himself. "Miss Lydia was a good woman," he said. "She used to be in the movies and she had more money than anybody else around here but she knew she was no different from people like me and never pretended she was. I owed her. When you said the one that beat her to death was in that Caddy I, well, I lost it for a minute. I never seen Jessie so mad at me as she got when she heard what I done. I had to bring the son of a bitch down." He crossed his legs and leaned forward in the chair. "You knew it was Stacy in there?"

"Knew is too strong a word," Loren said. "I'd begun to suspect. Remember when you were driving us out to the college and Lewis and I were reconstructing the murder? I said

206

after Lydia was dead the killer must have looked around the basement and noticed the audiocassette box lying on the bench on the other side of the exercise room. That was a small box. Very few people would have been cool and perceptive enough to have noticed it after committing a brutal murder. Veteran cops develop perceptive instincts. That was one pointer. There was a bigger one."

"Not that I could see," Wright said.

"You weren't there to see it. Whoever the murderer was, he or she had to have known the alarm system code at Lydia's house. Very few people knew that but Stacy was one of them. Last night when Heather was arrested I saw him deactivate the system when they opened the door to take her downtown. Remember this morning when the cop who was watching the house told us Stacy had taught him the code?"

"Sure I remember. Why couldn't Miss Lydia's bodyguard have given him the numbers?"

"He could have and I assumed he had just as you did," Loren said. "Until I began thinking hard about Stacy. That was when I remembered he'd said Sunday night that he'd need to come to the house and ask Lydia about her access card to the executive entrance. Probably it was on that visit that he asked about her security system and she showed him the code. I also remembered how Heather had described the man who whacked her in the Nature's Ovens lot as rather small, which is exactly what Stacy was. Of course none of this was proof but it did start me thinking."

There was another rap and the next moment the door was flung back and Lewis stood in the opening. "You decent?" He edged into the room and stepped aside to make room for the other visitor behind him.

Heather came in, still limping a little but without a cane, and made her way to Loren's bed and sat on its edge and held his hand to her lips. "I'll never have the right words . . ." He felt her tears on his hand. "If there's any good I do for others with the rest of my life it's because you saved me."

Her gratitude made him uncomfortable. He was tempted to remind her that her life had never been in danger because Wisconsin had no death penalty but resisted.

"I lost hope," she said softly. "I was in despair. You didn't come to see me, I had no one to turn to. If I could have thought of a way to kill myself in that cell I would have done it. I'll never lose hope again. Thank you forever."

Wright seemed to sense that he was a fifth wheel in the conversation and stood up, nodding to Lewis to take his chair. "You got enough company for now," he said. "Guess I better head home and take my medicine from Jessie."

"I don't think you'll need a prescription for her medicine," Loren told him. "Thanks again."

Lewis cleared his throat and lowered himself into the hard chair. "Like an update on what's been happening?"

"I saw on the news that two FBI agents with serial killer expertise had flown in from Chicago and are working with you," Loren replied. "By now you must know a lot that the media don't."

"A hell of a lot," Lewis admitted. "Stacy's house was a treasure trove and so was Manya Wentz."

"I gather they were having an affair?"

"Have been for two years," Lewis said. "He didn't care squat for her, she was just a convenience for him."

"Did she know he was committing these murders?"

"Not so we can prove it. Her story is she only got suspicious when Stacy borrowed her Cad both Sunday around the time of Phil Clift's murder and Tuesday around the time of Lydia's. You know why he came over to Dennison Hall today, right?" Loren said nothing. "It was to take her into the

208

boonies and kill her. That stupid cop out at the house called in and told him we'd been out there looking at canes. The prosecutor and the guy he thought of as her defense lawyer, all cozied up and working together. The canes had nothing to do with nothing, I'll get to that later, but he panicked. Decided to eliminate Wentz. If he'd got her out of rehearsal five minutes sooner she'd be dead now. Don't count on her being grateful though. Those three slugs messed her up so bad she'll never lift an instrument again."

"If she was in it with him," Loren said, "that's worse punishment than a court would have given."

"All the evidence we've found says he was in it alone," Lewis told him. "I don't mean those deaths in the family back in the Sixties, like Gregory Dennison down South or Robin Thorn in North Dakota. They were probably just what they seemed but if they were anything different we'll never know and Stacy didn't have anything to do with them. The recent stuff we can tie him to."

"How?" Loren asked.

"We checked his leave records at the Department. He took vacation time the week last October when Luis Arrabal got shoved under that subway in New York and also the week back in December when the sister here almost got shoved. The FBI guys found a credit card in a phony name hidden with some other stuff at his house. The account shows he bought plane tickets from Milwaukee to New York and back both weeks. They also found a bunch of state-of-the-art bugging devices at his house, including one with fibers we can link with the baseboard in the Dennison Properties office at Nature's Ovens."

"So he had that office bugged," Loren said. "Then he would have known about that meeting with the bread company executives, the one where Clift took Leo McGuire aside afterwards and said he suspected him of embezzling."

"That's the main reason Stacy killed Clift when he did," Lewis told him. "A ready-made fall guy. He dropped in at Clift's office Friday, said he'd received an anonymous letter with some hard evidence that one of the honchos at Nature's Ovens was cooking the books and made an appointment to meet Clift late Sunday afternoon at the bread company office where they could go over the stuff in complete privacy. Stacy got there early, circled around until he saw Clift drive in, then came into the lot right after him and they went in the executive entrance together using Clift's access card."

"Then that explains the attack on Heather five nights before Clift was murdered," Loren said. "Knowing he was going to commit the murder in that office, Stacy put on a dark outfit and ski mask, took a crowbar and paid that late night visit to remove the bug so his squad wouldn't find it later. And you, Heather, happened to pick that night to visit the plant and ran into him. If he'd recognized you he'd have killed you on the spot. You were next on his list." He struggled to sit up. Heather released his hand, arranged the pillows under his head and sat again on the bed's edge. "You came here to make yourself a target," he went on, "and you came within an inch of getting killed more than once. Stacy never intended to kill Lydia Tuesday. He wasn't a lawyer. He probably didn't know about the new codicil and certainly didn't work out the legal consequences if you should be convicted of Lydia's murder. He was out to kill you."

Heather's eyes widened through the moisture that filmed them. "Oh no," she said softly. "I never meant anyone to get hurt or die for me, but Lydia of all people . . ." Tears poured from her and she groped for his hand. Loren fumbled for the box of tissues on his bed table and thrust a wad of them between her fingers.

"We misread the evidence at the crime scene," he said when her trembling had subsided. "Stacy went out in Manya Wentz's Cadillac, parked a quarter mile away and sneaked onto the grounds. Whatever weapon he intended to use he had with him. He figured you were still more or less immobile after getting whacked, he knew Lydia's exercise routine and he had learned from her how to bypass the alarm system. Any fool with a coat hanger could have gotten past the latched gate in the privacy fence and into the pool yard. He peeks through the fence, sees and hears Lydia swimming her laps. That tells him his timing was right: he can slip past her, across the pool yard and into the house through the basement door, which is closed but not locked because she expects to go straight back into the basement when she's through. This is how he gets into the exercise room. Knowing the alarm by-pass code, he punches in the numbers the moment he's inside the basement door. His plan is to make his way upstairs and through the house, find you, Heather, kill you, and leave the house by the front door, punching in the bypass code again of course on his way out.

"But then two things happen. He sees your cane lying on the exercise room floor, and Lydia comes in sooner than he expected. Whether she finished her laps or sensed an intruder and came in to hit the panic button on her pager we'll never know. He sees her in the doorway. Grabs the cane. Runs after her, although again he remembers to punch in those bypass numbers before chasing her out into the pool yard. He catches her before she can dive into the pool. Starts bludgeoning her with the cane. She gets confused and blindly stumbles back into the basement. He's right behind her, punches in the code again, and finishes her on the basement floor before she can reach the pager. Then as he's looking around for evidence he might have left behind he notices the audiocassette box with the name Shostakovich on it, gets spooked because he drove out there in a car with a KOVICH license plate, and either puts it back on the shelves or takes it away with him."

"He took it with him," Lewis said. "Wentz told us she found it under the driver's seat on the floor of the Cad this morning."

"So you see," Loren said softly to Heather, "you escaped by the skin of your teeth three times. Once in New York, twice here."

"The FBI found a sort of diary he was keeping on the computer at his house," Lewis went on. "He thought he'd erased it but the feds have a computer program that's pretty good at bringing back erased material from a disk. We have it now. If he hadn't killed himself we would have nailed him with it. Unless that slimeball Unger got it suppressed or something."

"But why was he killing all these people?" Heather insisted. "He—had no stake in the trust, he wasn't a beneficiary, he wasn't related to any of us . . ."

"The answer was on his computer," Lewis said. "The whole plan. He never intended to kill Laura Yates, because she's dying already in Pinecrest Nursing Home, or Lydia or Ward Dennison either, because they were old and he figured nature would do those jobs for him. His targets in Dennison were first Phil Clift, then Professor Pardee at the college. When you came to town he decided to save Pardee for a bit and do you while you were reachable."

"But Charles Pardee isn't a beneficiary . . ." Heather protested.

That was the moment when light broke on Loren in the shadowed dimness, dazzling him. "Angela," he said, softly but with total certainty. "She was the key to it." Remembering how her dark beauty had bewitched him at Lydia's reception, he could almost understand how a man like Stacy, middle-aged and lonely like Loren himself, might have been overwhelmed.

"Right. After he killed Pardee he planned to court and marry her—having first made her a richer woman of course—and share the wealth himself. He was a man of faith, he believed absolutely that Angela wouldn't be able to resist him, and he staked everything on that faith."

"That's insane." Heather spoke with a sort of quiet fury.

"Yeah, I suppose Unger would have argued an insanity defense for him. You should read what he wrote on his computer about her. Classic obsession stuff. Too bad he lost faith and hope and ate his gun, isn't it, Sister? I bleed for the son of a bitch."

"Sister," Loren repeated dully. It was the second time Lewis had called her that, and the meaning of the fact suddenly came home to him. "You know then . . ."

"Domjan and I were playing phone tag all day. He caught me a few hours ago. I wish you'd have said something sooner, Professor."

"I couldn't," Loren said. "I knew she was innocent and thought it would hurt her. Forgive me?"

"Yeah, what the hell," Lewis growled. "The media would have been all over us even worse if they'd known she was a nun . . . God, we were all so blind, so wrong. That missing cane from Almon's box . . ."

"Yes, what about the cane?" Loren demanded.

"If I hadn't been in the military and overseas in 1964 when Almon died I'd have known," Lewis said. "Any old-timer around here could have told me. Pop cleared it up when I dropped by his room awhile ago to see how he's doing. Lydia had that cane put in the coffin with her husband. It's been in the family burial vault for the past thirty years . . . Let's see, is there anything I've left out?"

"Not you so much as Stacy," Loren answered. "There's another beneficiary here in Dennison that I gather wasn't on his hit list. How do you account for the absence of Clayton Brean?"

"Because Stacy was blackmailing the fat fool," Lewis said. "I told you we'd never know the truth about those deaths in the family back in the Sixties but there's one we know a hell of a lot about now. Brean's mother, the one who went over a cliff in 1970 when her brakes failed. Stacy went back into that case on his own and found what the staties missed back then. Little Clayton was in prep school back east when his mother bought it but he had a classmate and the classmate had a big brother and the big brother had connections. Jesus, a 17-year-old kid with no underworld experience arranging for a mob hit and getting away with it . . . Stacy dug up enough evidence to reopen the case. We found it squirreled away at his house. He was using it to squeeze Brean for inside poop about what was happening in the inner circle that ran the trust. Also for money. Every time he killed one of the other beneficiaries, Brean got richer and Stacy could squeeze him for more."

"No wonder he wanted to keep Brean alive for awhile," Loren said. "But there was another reason too. I knew instinctively Brean was tied to that attack on me Sunday morning when Lydia told me it was his car with the JSBACH license we saw when you drove me back to the Cheese Country Inn Sunday night. In case you didn't know, he took the room next to mine. So his James Bond antics tied him to Faith Family and Freedom and you've just tied him to Stacy."

"That James Bond crack may be truer than you realize," Lewis said. "When I had my little fireside chat with Brean tonight I got the distinct impression he felt he had sort of a license to kill you if God gave him the chance. I have a hunch Sister Heather isn't the only one in this room who played in luck."

"I still don't see how Stacy is connected with the attack on me," Loren said.

"Brean cleared that up nicely," Lewis explained. "No one else in town knew Heather was a nun but Stacy knew it from when he'd stalked her in New York and tried to kill her but missed. And of course he knew Brean was ass-deep in this Faith and Family organization. When Sister Heather came out here and her engagement to you was announced, he didn't know what it meant. Was it some kind of legal maneuver, or was she giving up being a nun and getting married for the money, or what? So his first move was a lateral pass. He let drop to Brean he had confidential information she was a nun. Brean didn't know how to handle the news either but he had some pals in the organization keep an eye on you back home and when you came into Wisconsin he had those old witches climb on your tail. The attack on you in the thunderstorm was a fluke. The biddies saw a God-given chance to strike a blow for faith, freedom and family and they took it." The prosecutor tried to stifle a grin. "They finally got out of that farmer's pasture and told Brean what you did to them yesterday and Brean told me tonight. There won't be any charges filed. Trust me."

"You're not going to charge him with paying to have his mother go over a cliff?"

"What's the use?" Lewis growled. "It happened almost twenty-five years ago, some of the evidence Stacy dug up would never be admitted in court, Unger would put his mother on trial and have Brean claim she beat him or raped him or whatever. I took Mr. Blubberbutt aside and made a private deal with him. I don't bring any charges against him or the old ladies, they don't bring any charges against you, but if that Faith Family and Freedom gang do anything in this area that doesn't set right with me, even if it's legal, all bets are off. Stacy's evidence gets mysteriously sent to the media, I get put under intense pressure to try Brean for conspiracy to commit murder. Let him worry about that the rest of his life. Might sweat some lard off him."

"That," Loren said weakly, "is a gross abuse of prosecutorial discretion."

"Sue me," Lewis grinned, and pushed out of the hard chair. "I have to tuck Pop in for the night. Drop by my office when they let you out of here." He waved, left the room and eased the door shut behind him.

Loren and Heather were alone in the dim cube lit only by a nightlight. Muted bells went *ting ting* in the corridor. A nurse's soft footsteps passed the closed door. Within the room the only sounds were Heather's muffled sobs.

"I did kill her," she said. "I blamed myself last night and now I know I'm more to blame than I thought yesterday . . . She died horribly for me and her money is mine now."

"Part of you wants to believe it was all meant to happen the way it did," Loren said, "and the other part understands what that would mean about the nature of whatever runs the universe. You can't accept the idea of yourself as God's favorite and Lydia as garbage but you can't accept what happened as blind chance either. Is that it?"

"You don't know how close I am to jumping out that window," she whispered.

Loren squeezed her hand tighter as if to hold her by force at his bedside. "Don't try it," he suggested. "First of all the window's unopenable and shatterproof, and besides you'd leave a worse legal mess behind than there is already. There'd be lawsuits over Lydia's estate well into the next century. I'm afraid you have to live awhile. At least until you've decided where all your new-found wealth goes if you do kill yourself."

"I know," she said. "I've thought about it a little. With Lydia dead the trust terminates and I'm a few months short of thirty so I haven't violated the restriction, I'm still a beneficiary. That means I'll wind up with the share of the principal that generated my income plus the fifty percent of the principal that generated Lydia's. That's an incredible amount of money. I still can't believe it's going to be mine. I . . . can't accept what had to happen to make it mine."

"You can't undo it either," Loren reminded her.

"I can use some of the money to support what Lydia believed in," she said. "Music is important too. I won't leave this town to rot. The rest of the money will support the shelter, maybe let me start the same sort of shelters in other cities."

"Remember the language of the codicil," Loren reminded her. "You're not obligated to spend a penny on philanthropy. You could walk away from, well, from all your past life and have every luxury you've ever dreamed of and no one could stop you."

"Even if I do give up being a nun do you honestly think I could spend a penny of that money on myself after all this horror?" she demanded.

"Most people could," he answered. "Not you. If I understand you at all you'll continue to live for others no matter what you decide you believe but I have no idea what belief you have left."

A cocoon of silence enveloped them for what might have been an hour. Then Heather stirred. "Loren?" she whispered. "Are you awake?"

"I'm fine," he said drowsily.

"Before you went to law school did you ever happen to read *Antigone*?"

"I've read it more recently than that." Seven years ago he had encountered a sociopath who borrowed from Sophocles' ancient drama in devising a plot to kill another sociopath. He knew that if he started telling her that story he would still be talking at dawn.

"There's a line from that play I've never been able to forget," she said. "Do you remember what she says when they're taking her to be buried alive?"

"Frankly, I don't," Loren admitted.

" 'Not to hate with those who hate, but to love with those who love, I was born.' " She recited the words with awe as if they were part of a ritual that meant more to her than her own life. "When Antigone said that . . . I still believe she was . . . how can I say it? . . . going with the grain of the universe and not against it. That may be the only faith I have left."

"More than I have," Loren said. "But even going against the grain of the universe, if that means anything, it's a good way to live. Whatever else you've lost, don't lose that."

"Thanks." She looked up at him and there was a new peacefulness in her features as if a crisis had passed. "I'd better go. It's probably after midnight and we both need rest." She began to rise from the hard mattress.

"Where are you staying?" Loren asked.

"That's funny. When they let me out of jail I called the Cheese Country Inn and they gave me the same room you had. I know I have to stay in town awhile, find a good lawyer to straighten out the estate."

"Also to run interference for you with the media," Loren said, "until the feeding frenzy's over."

"Mr. Fraser's going to handle that for a few days. Do you know how long you'll be in the hospital?"

"The doctor thinks I'll be out tomorrow morning. Day after tomorrow if it's not midnight yet."

"I could have another suite reserved for you," she said shyly. "Not that I want you to get the wrong idea."

"The wrong idea was the farthest thing from my mind." Loren remembered where he had heard that line before and laughed and she remembered then and laughed with him, very soft laughter so as not to disturb sleeping patients but rich and deep and full. She sidled to the head of the bed and they embraced. "I'll never forget you," she whispered, and slipped from his arms and out of the room.

He was alone. He lay in the hooded darkness and tried to sleep and wondered if loneliness was the shape of the rest of his life. How did he know Val was still involved with that new man? How did he know she wouldn't take him back? They hadn't exchanged a word in two years. He could pick up the phone on the bed table this minute, connect with his long distance carrier, punch in her number that he still knew by heart. No. He couldn't do that. Not at this hour. Not when she might be sleeping in another man's arms. Better to wait till morning, leave a message on her answering machine after she'd gone to the office. Would she return his call if he did? Start over with him after he had hurt her so deeply? Val, Heather, someone he might meet tomorrow or next week, no one ever again. Eeny meeny miny mo. Fate, chance, purpose, genes, choice?

When he could endure it no longer he rang for the night nurse and asked for a sedative and after a while, like a bubble blown from a child's pipe, his consciousness dissolved and there was rest.